If Things Were Made to Last Forever

Stories by
Michael C. Keith

ISBN: 978-0-9904872-8-9

Printed in the United States of America

This book is a work of fiction. The characters, names, and plots are entirely a product of the author's imagination. Any resemblance of the characters or incidents in this book to real life persons or events is unintentional and purely coincidental.

Stories in this volume first appeared in *Smokebox, McStorytellers, Literary Brushstrokes, Short-Humour, Festival Writers, The Penmen, The Literary Yard, Were-Traveler, Jitter Press, Fiction on the Web, Commonline Journal, Blue Hour Magazine, Clever Magazine, Calamities Press,* and *Boston Literary Magazine.*

Cover photo: *Paradox Lost* by Glenn Bowie
Cover Design: Christopher Reilley

Big Table Publishing Company
Boston, MA
bigtablepublishing.com

Also by Michael C. Keith

The Near Enough
The Collector of Tears
Everything is Epic
Sad Boy
Of Night and Light
Hoag's Object
And Through the Trembling Air
Life is Falling Sideways
Norman Corwin's 'One World Flight' (with Mary Ann Watson)
The Radio Station
Sounds of Change (with Christopher Sterling)
Radio Cultures
The Quieted Voice (with Robert Hilliard)
The Next Better Place
Dirty Discourse (with Robert Hilliard)
The Broadcast Century (with Robert Hilliard)
Queer Airwaves (with Phylis Johnson)
Talking Radio
Waves of Rancor (with Robert Hilliard)
Voices in the Purple Haze
The Hidden Screen (with Robert Hilliard)
Signals in the Air
Radio Programming
Global Broadcasting Systems (with Robert Hilliard)
Radio Production
Broadcast Voice Performance

Acknowledgments

As usual I wish to offer a heartfelt thank you to my exceptional readers: Nicki, Chris, and Susanne. Oh yes, and to Robin, who never ceases to inspire appreciation in her countless authors. This has become old hat, guys.

I'd like to dedicate this collection to the independent presses, such as Big Table Publishing, that serve as a lifeline for so many talented writers who otherwise would not see their work in print.

Table of Contents

The idea of eternity is exhausting.
~ Henny Youngman

(S)elective Memory

I never deny; I never contradict; I sometimes forget.
~ Benjamin Disraeli

Governor-elect Emil Frost slipped on the remnants of a fried pickle and slammed his head against the cement steps leading from his campaign headquarters. After a struggle, he managed to stand up, but then his world went dark. When he regained consciousness, strangers surrounded him.

At first the group frightened him. He didn't grasp the nature of their expressions. They seemed otherworldly and exotic to him. However, gradually he came to realize that he was being looked upon with great concern and curiosity. *Who are they?* he wondered, *and where am I? Who am I?*

Emil tried desperately to recall his identity and the specifics that had brought him to what was obviously a hospital. When he attempted to speak, all he could muster was a dry whisper. "What... ? Who... ?"

A grey-haired man, with a stethoscope dangling from his neck smiled at him reassuringly. "I'm Doctor Williams, the attending neurologist here at Westgate. You've had an accident and have been unconscious for three days. Can you tell me who you are?"

Emil searched for his name, but drew a total blank.

A woman spoke: "You know me, I'm Catlin... your fiancé and campaign publicist." She bent over Emil and looked into his eyes tenderly. What she found in them was a complete lack of recognition.

"Do you recall your fall, Mr. Frost?" asked the doctor. "Or anything about what happened to you?"

Emil looked at the curious faces around the room and then returned his gaze to Williams. "No, I don't remember... *anything.* Who are these people? Why are they here? Should I know them?"

"That's okay, Mr. Frost. Your type of brain trauma often results in temporary amnesia."

Emil reached for his head and for the first time noticed that he was attached to several wires that led to machines and an IV bag.

"We're keeping close tabs on you, but I think we'll be able to liberate you from all this paraphernalia very soon," said Williams.

The woman who called herself Catlin drew close to his face. "Look at me, babe. You know *me*."

"Please, Miss Gearhart. We shouldn't pressure Mr. Frost. It's better to give him time to gain back his memories than try to impose them on him. What you say could actually confuse him and block his ability to recollect. I know you don't want to hamper his recovery."

"No, of course not. Why would you think that?"

"I'm just saying that this is a lot for him to absorb all at once."

Another man said, "Okay then. Let's let the boss have some time to himself. It's been a real shock for him. Don't worry. He'll land the plane without casualties. We'll come back later. What say you to that, folks?"

"Fine," said Catlin, sounding resigned. "Love you, hon."

The man who called him "boss" led the small group out of the room, leaving only Dr. Williams behind.

"Why don't you shut your eyes and relax," he said to his patient. "Don't force yourself to remember things. They'll come drifting back on their own, and probably sooner than you think. I'll be back to check on you in a couple hours, Mr. Frost."

Once alone, Emil did as the physician suggested, and closed his eyes. After what felt like a long and arduous struggle to seize upon anything, something, from his past. Emil began to regain images of himself in a variety of situations. The first sustained recollection had him seated in a car–his car–sucking on a joint, while "Reelin' in the Years" by Steely Dan blasted from the tape deck. His college girlfriend, Amanda, was next to him, bouncing with the beat of the music.

"Give me a toke. You're smoking it all, Emil."

Emil took a long drag and passed the weed to her.

The scene suddenly shifted to Amanda crying and informing Emil that she was pregnant with his baby.

"Is it mine? I mean… well, you've been with other guys since we met."

"Yeah, but I'm pretty sure it's yours."

"Okay, so what do you want to do, babe?

"I guess I could get an abortion."

"That makes sense," said Emil, staring blankly at the gently swaying crystal dangling from his rearview window.

Another memory took center stage in Emil's head. In this one, he and several others were marching in front of the state capitol. Their placards revealed they were protesting the prevalence of handguns. A confrontation soon erupted between firearm supporters and the protesters. A bloodied Emil was dragged to a waiting police car, all the while shouting anti-gun slogans.

As soon as the police sirens sounded, the scene changed and Emil was arguing with his father at a family barbeque. The senior Mr. Frost was shouting, "You can't tell me it's right for two men, or even two women, to get married! That's a sin against nature and God. It ain't right. Marriage is for a man and woman, *period*. It's to have kids and a family. That's what the Bible says, and it's the law. It's the way it's always been and should always be. Same-sex marriage, my ass! It's… well, damn disgusting! Makes me sick!"

"That's primitive thinking, Dad. If two people love each other and want to be together, why shouldn't they be allowed to marry? I thought we lived in a free country?"

"Marriage is sacred, and it's not for queers and deviants."

"That's ridiculous!"

"You're ridiculous, Emil! All your views are just plain *un-*American. Where's your patriotism? I suppose we should let all the wetbacks come into this country illegally, too, right? And we should increase welfare for all the crack heads in the ghetto while we're at it."

"Jesus, Dad, you're worse than Archie Bunker. Not everybody in the ghetto is an addict. Most are just poor, underprivileged people trying to survive!"

Emil was suddenly roused from his ruminations by the voice of the woman who had earlier claimed to be Caitlin, his fiancé.

"We're back honey. I don't care what Dr. Williams said. I think we can help you remember things. We're getting married right after your inauguration."

"Inauguration?" asked Emil.

"Yes, my old friend," chimed the man. "I'm Barry Finn, your campaign manager. You're going to be our next governor!"

"Governor! How can I be governor if I can't remember anything?"

"Doesn't matter, we'll figure something out."

Emil was delighted; his memories all made sense now. *I must have spent my life trying to change the world for the better, and as soon as I get elected, I can really make it happen!* but before he could speak, the man who called himself Barry Finn declared with a glance at Caitlin, "Yessiree, Bob, the GOP has got itself a winner in Emil Frost!"

Material Coping

Chico and Mary Lavoie had four sons, and in as many years they had none.

Ronny was their youngest, and he was the first to go. A terminal disease claimed him at age 32. He had smoked two packs of Marlboros a day for most of his life, despite his parent's constant pleading that he stop. To cope with their devastating loss, the Lavoies purchased matching Rolexes.

Less than six months after Ronny's demise, Carlos crashed his motorcycle into the back of a trash removal truck. His injuries did him in two days later. The Lavoies were shocked as well as forlorn, since their son had always taken the greatest of precautions on his Yamaha Stryker. To deal with the tragedy, the distraught parents bought a 28-foot Chris Craft cabin cruiser.

The next year brought even more pain to Chico and Mary when their second born drowned while swimming in the local quarry. It was not just devastating, it was completely unexpected: Barry had been an award-winning member of the Y's swim team. To handle their despair, the Lavoies added a media center to their house.

When their last surviving child, Carson, died in a construction accident just 13 months later, the Lavoies again knew they had to do something to come to terms with their crushing grief. After considering numerous possibilities, they realized that their grieving had left them broke.

Breakfast for Cassie

*If the doors to perception were cleansed, everything
should appear as it is, infinite.*

~ William Blake

Cassie felt the sounds that the Object made: *"Guloop has sas, hone."*
The Object repeated the sounds, *"Guloop has sas, hone."* Sometimes the
sounds the Object made hurt her ears. Other times the sounds made
her lean forward because they were so quiet.

"See what Mommy has, honey," said Cassie's mother, Mary.

Her seven-year-old daughter looked at her blankly.

"Time for your cereal, baby."

The Object placed something near Cassie's face. It contained a
familiar smell.

"Here you go, love. Nice oatmeal with raisins. Good and hot. Do
yummy-yummy for Mommy, okay, doll baby?"

The Object made more sounds: *"Sabid foof madef here."*

Cassie felt the thing the Object held touch her lips. She turned
away abruptly, making the room spin for her.

"No, *no*, Cassie. It's good. Eat, honey, *please*. Open up for Mr.
Spoon."

The Object pressed the thing into Cassie's mouth. It felt sharp
and stung a little. She swallowed and wanted more.

"Kaslep there foto minga," sounded the Object, and Cassie made
open again.

"Good girl. That's nice. Big open. Nice *big* open," added Mary,
enthusiastically.

Cassie reached for the Object's dangling auburn strands and
grabbed at them. The Object's narrow orbs danced in and out. Black
lines swayed in the bright space behind the Object. Cassie liked the
movement of the lines and bounced back and forth with them.

"Seepod gofub tree terup," said the Object, moving the thing to and
fro to catch her daughter's mouth.

The Other Object entered and made sounds too.

16

"How's Daddy's little girl? Having breakfast?" asked Mary's husband.

The first Object always seemed to understand what the other Object said, and responded, "*Se Da pato... Da,*" and held up two fingers.

"Two spoonfuls," said Mary. "But we're not done yet, are we, Cassie?"

The Other Object disappeared, and Cassie felt the thing the Object held slide from her openness.

"Good girl," said Mary, pushing her hair back from her eyes and drawing sticky morsels from it.

Cassie liked the fluttery things that dropped onto the black lines in the bright space to the Object's back.

"All done," said Mary, content that her daughter had eaten enough.

As Cassie watched the Object rise and vanish, she felt a long succession of rumbles that were followed by a series of colorful flashing lights. Her hand tensed to a claw and floated above her head.

"*Ofub Cas sesup klim,*" said the Object reappearing before her.

The fluttery things in the bright space had Cassie's rapt attention as something was pressed against her lips.

"Time for lunch, sweetie. Open wide!" said Mary, smiling lovingly at her daughter.

The fluttery things moved around the dark lines in the bright space and made Cassie smile.

"*Yes*, it *is* Mommy, honey... *yes!*" said Mary, delighted.

Facial Hare

I heard a sudden cry of pain!
There is a rabbit in the snare.
~ James Stephens

Cyril Huguenot was diagnosed with Congenital Hypertrichosis or Ambrose Syndrome, as it was more commonly called. Not long after reaching adulthood, he noticed that his beard was growing more rapidly than it ever had. He would shave in the morning but by noon had a growth far exceeding what was known as a five o'clock shadow. The thickness of his beard grew to the point that he had to cut it with scissors before attempting to use a conventional razor.

After fighting to control it for several years, he decided to let it grow into a beard–let it be what it clearly wanted to be. But even that didn't work, and he found himself chopping it back with alarming frequency. Then he noticed that the hair on the top of his head was also growing at greater speed. Whereas in the past, he would visit Supercuts every four or five weeks, he was now going in two-week intervals. He was even sprouting hair on his forehead and cheeks.

"What's going on with you, Cy?" asked his wife, Audrey. "You're beginning to look like Big Foot."

"Thanks for that. Makes me feel a whole lot better. You know I have a condition."

"Sorry, hon. I know. *But...* "

To compound Cyril's escalating anxiety, his hair had become streaked with white... and soon was completely gray.

"Markey thought you looked like a bunny. That's what he told his friends," said Audrey.

"So that's why all the kids kept coming over."

"What are you going to do? It's beginning to look real freaky. Don't they say anything about it at work?" she inquired.

"Sure they do. They've nicknamed me *Harvey*. You know, after the movie with James Stewart."

18

"But no one could see that rabbit. It was invisible. That was the point of the story."

"Wish no one could see me."

"So what can you do? I know it's a disorder… Hyper-something, but they must have something better to treat it other than what you take. You can't go on looking this way. It's bizarre," protested Audrey.

"Ambrose Syndrome. It's called Ambrose Syndrome. I told you that before."

"I know. I said I was sorry, but it was never like this. It's obviously getting a whole lot worse."

"I've made an appointment with the doctor. I'm as upset about this as you are."

"You don't look quite as cute as you did. You're starting to look more like a wolf than a rabbit. You're beginning to scare the kids, Cy. Even Markey is afraid."

"Great, now my own little boy thinks I'm the boogeyman."

The following Monday, Cyril was at the doctor's office.

"Whoa, looks like your AS is on a tear," said Dr. Ferris, upon seeing his patient. "Have you been taking your anti-androgens?"

"Ask my wife. I don't think I have any testosterone left."

"Sorry to hear that. It can be frustrating, I know, but reducing testosterone is about the only option available to treat your particular medical issue. Let's increase the dose of your meds for a month and see if that slows things down. I think it might."

"Hey, may as well. My sex drive is gone now anyway. Can't get any worse, I suppose."

"We could take you off the anti-androgens entirely and see what happens," suggested Ferris.

"Man, I'm afraid I might end up looking like Chewbacca if I stop completely, doc. Scaring the hell out of kids already, including my own son. I don't know. Let's try increasing the prescription."

"Okay, we'll give it a month. In the meantime, I'll do some research to see if there are any AS trials going on that you might participate in to see if we can get this under control."

"If we can't, I may as well join the circus, because I sure can't have a normal life looking like this."

Cyril was back in Dr. Ferris' office four weeks later, and despite the medicine boost, his problem had continued to worsen. Hair now covered his entire body, and the density of it obscuring his facial characteristics and making him barely recognizable. His wife did her best to deal with the situation but was understandably upset by what was happening to her husband. Meanwhile, their son had grown increasingly reluctant to be near Cyril, and that pained him greatly.

"I'm sorry, Mr. Huguenot, but I have been unable to find any AS trials, and I'm really at a loss as to what to do to reverse or even slow the growth of your fu… ah, hair."

"It *is* fur. C'mon, doc, say it… thick animal *fur*. I don't look human any more. I frighten myself when I look in the mirror."

"How do you feel otherwise? Are there any other physical symptoms?" asked Ferris, moving the tresses that covered Cyril's eyes in order to shine a light in them.

"Other than feeling like a wooly mammoth? No, not really."

What Cyril didn't admit was that he had become increasingly restless and unable to sleep. During the last couple of weeks, he found himself in his backyard staring at the moon. As it grew full, he became more agitated. At the same time, he experienced a sharp increase in his auditory and olfactory senses, and every noise or movement in the darkness made him jump in fear.

"I think we need to run more tests. AS is not uncommon, but your case is pretty exceptional, to say the least. I'd like to admit you to the hospital after Easter. Let's say next Tuesday. You'll only be there overnight."

Cyril reluctantly agreed to his doctor's plan and returned home feeling that his life would never be normal again, if it had ever been.

By Saturday, Cyril had not slept a wink, and an inexplicable urge was beginning to take hold of him. By evening, the strange and wild impulse drove him from the house. In the bright light of the full moon, he found himself slipping into the homes of his sleeping neighbors to sate his overpowering compulsion.

After a few hours, Cyril felt his insistent needs met and hopped from the window of the last home on his block. He returned to his own house where he finally fell into a deep, restorative sleep.

In the morning, shrieks echoed through the neighborhood. Children had discovered the largest Easter baskets they had ever seen.

Individual Concerns

"Do you *not* recognize the absurdity of human existence... the folly of it all?" inquired Wilson. But before Bellows had a chance to respond, Wilson continued, "We're spinning through space on a piece of rock with other space objects flying around us... "

"Yes, but let's... "

"Both the Big Bang Theory and the notion of a God are really impossible to verify... "

"There's the... "

"And at any moment we could be disintegrated by an errant asteroid... "

"Sure, that's possible, but... "

"And every few seconds, somebody is killed by someone else... "

"Can we... ?"

"A country attacks another country every other day... "

"Look, we should... "

"Disease ravages our population... "

"Shut up, and let me say something!"

"Fine... fine, so what do you have to *say?*"

"Are we going to order dessert, or what?"

Private Activities

Things have come to a pretty pass when [man] is
allowed to invade the sphere of private life.
~ Lord Melbourne

"Somebody hid a minicam in the President's bedroom!" whispered White House staffer Scott Piffin to his girlfriend.

"You're kidding! What did they record? Who did it? Why... ?" asked Christy Houser, excitedly.

"Whoa! I've no idea. I just overheard a couple Secret Service guys talking in the hall of the East Wing when I was on my way to Skipper Larson's office."

"Did you tell him what you heard?"

"No, I wasn't sure what to do, but I think I'll call him later. Maybe just talk to him tomorrow."

"You're going to wait? Shit, this is huge! Call him now," pleaded Christy, slipping out of bed and putting on her robe.

"Okay, but I have to be careful. You just don't go repeating something the Secret Service says in confidence."

Scott swung around and sat on the edge of the bed in his boxers. He hit the speed dial on his iPhone and it rang twice before Skipper Larson answered.

"Hey, Skip. How you doing? Listen, I heard something today that I probably shouldn't be repeating. But it's got a lock on my thoughts, and I figured I'd... well, tell you what I heard."

"Okay, shoot, my friend," said the voice on the other end of the line.

"Sure... right. Well, I was heading to your office this afternoon, and I passed a couple of Secret Service guys. I couldn't help but overhear one say to the other that the President's bedroom was bugged."

"Huh?"

"Yeah, POTUS' bedroom was bugged. That's what I heard."

"Shit, you got to be kidding! How the hell... ?"

"No idea. That's why I had to share it with you. If that's a fact, then this is monster stuff, right?"

"Fuck… no kidding!"

"What should we do? Pretend we know nothing? I mean it really doesn't concern us, right?"

"Yeah, let the guys in black deal with it. But I'd sure like to know what was recorded and who did it. Whether the bugger is going public with what he recorded. I'll see if I can find out anything without raising a flag."

"Would you tell me if you do, Skip?"

"Sure. You let me know, too."

Despite the stealthy efforts of both men, no further information about the bugging turned up. But speculation between Scott and Skip about the content of the alleged recordings covered a wide swath.

"Jeez, what if they were having kinky sex? Imagine if that got on YouTube. A quadrillion hits in seconds," offered Scott.

"Or drugs. What if they were smoking pot or doing lines? Holy crap! That would be the biggest scandal in history," countered Skip.

"Maybe they were fighting? Cursing each other out?"

"Cross dressing? Watching pornos? Dirty dancing? No way! *Way?*"

"Wonder why it hasn't gotten out? Who the hell made it into the President's private quarters to bug the bedroom?"

"Got to be an insider. There are surveillance cameras everywhere but in the private quarters, so it may not be easy to nail the culprit."

"My Secret Service contact denied the bugging. But he blinked. I mean his expression changed for a second, so I'm sure something is going on. This would be the biggest breach in White House security ever."

"Can you keep pressing him on it, Skip?"

"I'll let it go for a couple days, and then I'll approach him again. He lives in the building across from mine, and I see him a lot. I'll talk to him away from ground zero."

At 11 o'clock that Saturday night, Scott received a call that cleared up the mystery.

"My mole let the cat out of the bag, but he said he'd have to kill me if I said anything. So I'm saying the same thing to you."

"Understood," replied Scott, his heart rate accelerating.

"They bagged the dude. He was a new junior security guy. Guess the idiot was going to blackmail the Secret Service. Figured they would pay anything to keep from looking so bad. You know, *can't even protect POTUS in the White House*. Crap would really hit the fan."

"No kidding."

"Can't imagine anyone doing such a stupid thing though? As if there was a chance in hell he could get away with it."

"What about the recording? Did they get it?"

"Yeah, the fool had downloaded it on his laptop. Only about ten minutes' worth of boudoir activity."

"Oh my God! What was on it?"

"I don't think I should say. I shouldn't be telling you. You damn sure better not repeat this conversation. Shit, we shouldn't be talking on the phone. See you in the morning at Starbucks."

Before Scott could say anything else, Skip had hung up.

"So they caught the person who bugged the President?" asked Christy.

"Yeah, but I promised Skip I wouldn't repeat what he said."

"Are you kidding? I heard most of the conversation. So… ?"

Scott reluctantly filled Christy in on the contents of the phone call and made her swear to say nothing about it. He then attempted to go back to sleep, but his mind would not shut down, and he spent the night tossing and turning.

An hour before the alarm went off, Scott finally gave in to his insomnia. By 7:30 he had managed to clear most of the cobwebs from his head, and he made a beeline to the coffee shop. Skip was waiting.

"Hey, man, you don't look too chipper. Better get a double espresso," said Skip, sipping his latte.

"Couldn't sleep. Kept wondering what was recorded on… "

"Shh! Keep it down. This is beyond top secret."

"Sorry, so what was on it?" pressed Scott.

"You know, I think it's better if I say nothing more."

"What? You got to be shitting me, Skip."

"Look, this is very sensitive stuff. We're the only ones outside of the Service that knows this happened. They're not going to make any public statements about it. They're dealing with it internally."

"You got to tell me what was recorded. I know everything else. Was it sex? Were they getting high? What the hell… ?"

"I don't know if I… "

"Just tell me, for God's sake!"

"Okay, okay. But keep it down." Skip paused as if hoping something miraculous would intervene and save him from having to reveal the content of the recording.

"Well?" asked Scott impatiently. "It must have been something pretty damning or embarrassing."

"Yeah, not good. Not good at all," said Skip, finally speaking.

"C'mon, man! What were POTUS and the First Lady doing?"

"They were . . ."

"*Were* what?"

"They were eating… *McDonalds.*"

The Savior

There is something which excites compassion
in the very word... compassion.
~ Sydney Smith

Masao climbed the steep hill behind his family's hut to where he often spent hours looking out over the limitless savannah. When he reached the summit, he discovered a nest of black-tailed crakes. The chicks–three in all–pleaded with him to drop something, anything, into their gaping beaks. They appeared malnourished and one seemed on the verge of death.

The young Masai looked above to the outstretched limbs of the *Barringtonia pendula* expecting to see the parents of the baby birds. But all he saw were the abundant banana-shaped fruit dangling from the reddish-brown tree. Thinking their guardians had abandoned the tiny, fuzzy creatures after their fall to the ground, Masao decided to come to their rescue.

He climbed the low limb to where a clump of fruit hung. It was directly above the squawking fowl. *I will save you from your dire plight and free you from your pain*, he mumbled, removing a small blade from his belt. It took several swipes to cut through the thick stalk holding the produce. Finally, they fell to earth striking the black-tail crakes and crushing them.

"There," said Masao, pleased with his effort. "No more suffering."

Sochi Dog

Animals are such agreeable friends—they ask no
questions, they pass no criticisms.
~ T.S. Eliot

Zorya had survived by being the fastest dog in Sochi, Russia. This meant he was able to scour the garbage pails for sweet bones and sauce soaked stale breads before any of the other hundred or so canines that existed in the city. It was a hard life, but Zorya loved being near the Black Sea, and considered himself lucky to have so many good comrades among his fellow strays.

"Come Pavel, Mitya, and Bimka! Eat what is left of my scraps," barked Zorya to his closest friends, with whom he often shared his find.

Residents of Sochi had long tolerated the existence of the homeless canines, and some actually showed them kindness, especially the children. In the end, despite all of its many shortcomings, the coastal Russian municipality was home to the roving mutts.

Then, in 2008, the tranquility of the region was suddenly shaken with the beginning of huge road and building construction. Why this was happening was beyond the understanding of Zorya and his comrades, but some good fortune came with the giant trucks, towering cranes, and rumbling steamrollers—and thousands of workers.

A large number of the Zorya's canine tribe were rounded up and trained to keep intruders away from the various building sites. This meant that for first time the Sochi dogs did not have to scrounge for table scraps, since they were fed regularly for their services.

For five years, the dogs had shelter and enjoyed the kindness of their caretakers. But one day the work stopped and the construction equipment was taken away, along with fences that had contained them. The workers left, and the Sochi dogs were set free and left to return to their lives as scavengers.

"So be it," said Zorya to his mates. "We'll return to the life we had before. It wasn't as good as the one we've now lost, but it wasn't terrible."

"Close to it," whimpered Bimka.

"We still have each other, so it is *not* terrible," replied Zorya, placing his paw on the old hound's head.

"*Da*, we are a clan," added Pavel.

As their hunger grew, the dogs scurried about Sochi hunting through garbage for something edible. And as before, Zorya was always ahead of the other strays. To his surprise, he found more refuse than ever before. The builders had made many new structures to accommodate the needs of visitors, and this in turn produced a virtual overabundance of discarded consumables.

"It is better now than when we were guard dogs. We have our freedom and more leavings than ever before," noted Mitya, lapping up a glob of pork grease.

"Things keep getting better," declared Zorya.

But these good days for the Sochi strays were to be short lived.

Complaints from several officials of the Winter Games about the town's high derelict dog population weighed heavily on the mind of Sochi Mayor Sergey Rybkin. If the famous international athletic event were marred by problems, he would incur the wrath of the State Duma and probably find himself out of office and even working on a rock pile somewhere.

Rybkin's time in office had been marked with great success. During his tenure, the number of restaurants, stores, and hotels had multiplied. Sochi had taken on a more prosperous appearance, and the mayor prided himself on that transformation. He had become a rising star in the regional government and was looked upon with great favor by the Kremlin.

"The strays must be eliminated, or we will be ruined," he informed his wife, Olga.

"No, they cannot be harmed," she replied, horrified at the idea that the animals she loved would be mistreated.

Since she was a child, Olga had formed close alliances with many of the strays. She had fed and cared for them when they were sick or injured. Among her favorites was Zorya, who frequently visited her and her daughter, Anna.

"Moscow has given orders that they be exterminated. They are a public nuisance to the Games, because they frighten visitors. Vendors do not want them around their businesses. It is for the good of the town that the hounds either be driven out or put down. I have my orders, and there is nothing I can do."

Despite his family's protestations, Rybkin set about to implement the directives from the capital, which had recommended that the homeless dogs be poisoned in much the same way as diseased vermin were.

"But they are not rats!" protested Olga, when her husband admitted to the plan to dispatch the strays.

"They *are* to the businesses of the town and they *are* to our future... *my* future. If they are allowed to stay and roam free, it will be our ruin if someone is bitten. No, they must go!"

Three days later, animal exterminators from Rostov began to place deadly chemicals in the best-known feeding spots of the canine packs. Their actions did not escape the keen eyes of Zorya, who immediately spread word of the deadly initiative.

"Do not eat from the garbage. It will kill you," Zorya warned his mates.

"But why? It is what sustains us," replied the strays.

"They wish to remove us from Sochi by poisoning us."

"That cannot be. This is home to us just as it is to the humans."

"We are now considered a scourge because of the coming Games. They want us gone," continued Zorya.

"No, that's not it. This really is your scheme to keep all the scraps for yourself... and your dear comrades Bimka, Pavel, and Mitya," growled several of the canines.

"That is not true! You will die if you devour the garbage!" barked Zorya, as the pack dispersed.

His warning went unheeded, and within a matter of hours, several dogs had succumbed to the poison chemicals placed in neighborhood refuse containers and bags. Their carcasses were tossed onto trucks and quickly removed in the deep of night so as not to attract undue attention

"You were telling the truth. We have lost many comrades," admitted members of the stray community to Zorya.

As the dogs abandoned the urban streets for safer outlying areas, they noticed a caravan of large black cars streaming toward Sochi.

"It must be an important visitor," observed Pavel from a hilltop.

"Yes, someone of great importance," said Zorya, who then scampered down to the road and followed the vehicles as they entered town.

He made his way into the crowded village square to where the cars came to a stop. The assembled mass cheered loudly as a familiar figure took the stage and began to speak:

"Welcome, my fellow citizens and visitors from afar. As Mayor of Sochi, I am honored to introduce the Premier of the great Mother Land... "

It was at that point, Zorya decided to risk everything to show the dignitaries that stray dogs were not dangerous and were worth saving. He scampered up the stairs to the stage and ran to the dignitary, who was about to speak. When Rybkin spotted the canine, he attempted to wedge his body between himself and the Russian leader, but he was too late. By then, the Premier had started to pet Zorya, whose tail wagged enthusiastically.

"Leave him," shouted the high official to the mayor. "He is a good animal. Look how friendly he is. We must be kind to these beasts."

It had become well known to the Russian hierarchy that the project to exterminate the Sochi dogs was causing an outcry around the globe, and the Premier recognized the moment as an opportunity to reverse the negative image.

"You are my friend, doggy. Indeed, I will take you home with me," declared the Premier to the approving audience, as he lifted Zorya in his arms.

In the days that followed, the poison was removed from the Sochi garbage heaps and the strays were welcomed back into the village. Due to the press and social media, they had become as popular as the renowned athletes participating in the Games. Visitors from foreign lands adopted many, and the residents of the seaside Russian community treated the remaining dogs with increased charity. For the hounds of Sochi, it had become the best of all possible worlds.

Unfortunately, Zorya had met a different fate. Thirty kilometers away from Sochi, the Russian Premier had pushed him from his vehicle, saying, "Out, you flea-bitten mutt. You are lucky you have lived so long."

In the car immediately behind the Premier's, a thickset man heard the words coming through his earphone—and removed a pistol from a holster inside his coat.

Texting the Dead

There's a ghost in the new machine.
~ Tracy Kidder

Martha Lambert was devastated by the death of her husband of thirty-eight years, and for weeks she would not leave the house. Then suddenly her children noticed a remarkable change in her mood. She was bright and cheery and seemed almost like her old self.

"What's up, Mom?" asked Martha's youngest child, Carol. "You seem so much… "

"Better?" answered Martha.

"Yeah, I'd say," said Carol's older brother, Jonathan.

"Well, I feel much better, kids."

"Ah… why? I mean just yesterday you were so… "

"Miserable, Carol? Yes, I was, but then something changed that, and I'm really feeling… well, less depressed and lonely."

"It's so wonderful to see you like this, Mom. We were so worried about you. What happened?"

"A message," said Martha, smiling.

"Message? Who from?" asked Carol.

"Well, maybe you two better sit down."

Jonathan and Carol did as their mother suggested, taking a seat on the couch

"What's going on, Mom? This all sounds so mysterious."

"Your father… I got a text from your *father*," said Martha, her eyes welling up with tears of joy.

"Huh? A text? Mom, are you all right? Maybe we should take you to see the doctor."

"You've been under a lot of stress since dad died. It can cause you to imagine things," added Jonathan, looking at his mother with growing concern.

"I'm not going crazy, kids. I'm getting *texts* from your father," protested Martha.

"Look… get your coat, Mom. We'll take you to see someone to make sure nothing… "

"Yes, let's go right now. Maybe you've had a mini-stroke," appealed Jonathan.

"I'm not having hallucinations, for Heaven's sake! Your father really did send me a… "

"C'mon, Mom. We'll get you checked out," said Carol, fetching her mother's coat from the hall closet.

Suddenly Martha's cellphone began pinging and she looked at its screen.

"There, you two. *See!*" said Martha, smiling and holding her phone up for her children to see.

Their expressions instantly changed to one of incredulity as they read the text:

"Carol and Jonathan, mind your own damn business! Love, Dad."

A Short but Meaningless Life
or
A Millennial Saga

Billy Simpson had died at 27. He'd been born into a family of substantial wealth and privilege, affording him all the advantages one could imagine. While he failed to achieve distinction in prep school, due to low grades and a lack of athletic prowess, the Ivy's doors stood open to him because of his parent's prominence and eminent pedigree. However, Billy had decided against pursuing higher education in preference of a long-held plan. When he turned 21, a vast trust fund made it possible for him to do what he always wanted. He purchased an expensive condo overlooking the East River and set about to realize his unique goal. Six years later, after a relentless diet of fast food, video games, and 281-thousand cellphone texts, he let his 450-pound torso fall from his eleventh floor balcony.

The Boy Who Would Be Van Gogh

As if his whole vocation were endless imitation.
~ William Wordsworth

Nicholas Wacker began painting early. While other kids his age enjoyed the typical pursuits of boyhood, he spent his days in the local library poring over works of the great art masters. No artist captivated him more than Vincent Van Gogh. He loved the bold textures and vibrant colors and soon began emulating the artist's approach.

Initially his efforts were no more than a seven-year-old's attempt at copying something of which he had little grasp or understanding. Still his parents were pleased with his interest in painting and bought him everything he needed to fully explore it. The glint in his pale blue eyes when he took up a brush rewarded them a thousand fold. However, when they suggested he take lessons, he balked.

"I want to do it myself. I don't want a teacher," he answered with such determination and conviction that his parents relented.

Nicholas made rapid progress with his brushes, and soon relatives and family friends were taking notice of his ability. By his tenth birthday, some were of the mind he was a genuine prodigy. Nicholas felt the same.

"I can really make beautiful pictures, can't I, Mom?"

"You certainly can. Just like Van Gogh."

"Yes, just like Van Gogh," repeated Nicholas, enormously pleased with himself.

When Nicholas showed his rendition of *The Starry Night* to his 6th grade teacher, she first assumed it was a print of the world-renowned painting.

"That's one of my very favorite pictures, Nicky. Did your mother buy this print for you?"

"No, I painted it!"

"You painted it? Really?" replied Miss Harper, doubtfully.

"Run your finger over the trees. You can feel the oils. If you touch the star in the right corner, you can see that it's not really dry yet. I finished it this morning to bring to 'show and tell.'"

The skeptical teacher put her finger where Nicholas directed and was surprised to find that he was right.

"Well, that's… "

"See,I told you, Miss Harper. I'm working on Van Gogh's *Irises*. I'll bring it in Monday if you'd like to see it."

"Of course I'd like to see it, Nicky," said the astonished instructor.

At the end of the school day, Miss Harper called Nicholas's mother to tell her about Nicholas's wild claims about reproducing the work of the great painter.

"Yes, we know that Miss Harper. Nicholas has a unique talent and we're very proud of him."

"So the paintings are really his own work?"

"Oh, yes. He's been painting Van Gogh for several years."

"Have you shown his paintings to any art experts? It's quite extraordinary for a 12-year-old to accomplish such advanced work."

"No, but we're going to show his paintings to the public when he wants to, which we think will be sooner than later. Maybe in a year or so. He says he wants to paint *The Potato Eaters* and *The Night Café* next. When he's ready, we'll contact a gallery. Don't worry. We'll certainly invite you."

Three years later, Nicholas had reproduced more than 100 of Van Gogh's works and a gallery had agreed to offer him an exhibit. The Wackers' son had wanted to paint many more from the artist's canon before showing them, but his parents hoped sales from the exhibit might defray the looming cost of his college education.

"I don't want to go to college. I want to complete painting all of the Van Gogh oils there are. That is what I want to do. It's what I love doing."

Nicholas's obsession with the Dutch master had become a growing concern of the Wackers. While they were thrilled with their son's obvious talent, they saw in his single-mindedness a danger to his health. Nicholas had become very thin and his behavior had become erratic. Swings in his mood and his frequent periods of aloofness even put the Wackers at odds with one another. While his mother, Anna, felt her son was only exhibiting the common symptoms of incipient creative genius, his father, Ted, believed Nicholas was showing signs of mental distress.

"He should see a child psychologist. The boy has been so consumed with painting Van Gogh he's beginning to act like him. The next thing he'll do is cut off his ear."

Unbeknownst to the Wackers, their only child had been fighting the urge to do just that. At 19, he'd had his earlobe stretched to accommodate a plug, On two occasions he had removed it when overcome by the desire to slit the dangling lobe with an exacto knife. He had stopped at the very last second, knowing his parents would be appalled. Nonetheless, the urge continued to assert itself.

To placate his parents, Nicholas reluctantly agreed to display his work at a local gallery. While he had completed many of Van Gogh's better-known works, the gallery could only accommodate a third of them because of space limitations. It promoted the upcoming event widely, proclaiming Nicholas the virtual reincarnation of the famous 19th century artist. The opening attracted a large crowd, which included the prominent local art critic for the local newspaper, James Woodley.

"You'll be reviewed in the *Times*," squealed Mrs. Wacker, delighted by the attention her son was attracting.

Yet despite her high expectations, only two of Nicholas' paintings were sold.

"I think people don't recognize what an achievement these paintings are," bemoaned the gallery owner. "They think they're just copies of Van Gogh, but they don't realize what brilliance it took to make them. We'll sell more when people realize what we have here. I'm confident of that."

When the review of the show appeared the next day, expectations were lowered, if not dashed. In Woodley's words, "The exhibit is a carnival sideshow featuring the work of a freakishly talented young imitator. Nothing more, and perhaps a whole lot less. The young man should find another muse to inspire him, because his current one is merely channeling an already revered original."

While Nicholas paid little attention to the review, his parents were devastated and took the critic's comments to heart.

"Honey, why don't you try painting something else? Something your own. You're so talented, I bet you could create wonderful scenes from your own imagination."

"Mom is right, son. Invent work that is truly your own. You have such an enormous gift, and it might be gratifying for you to do work that's really yours," added Ted Wacker.

"You don't understand. I am doing what is mine. It reflects what is in my soul. Why would you want me to paint what isn't me?" shouted Nicholas, storming from his parent's house.

Nicholas wandered the city aimlessly, his thoughts swirling like the clouds that cast their shadows on the path before him. Gradually, the objects around him took on the famous qualities he so loved to emulate on his canvasses. After several hours of walking and thinking, he found himself at the city's renowned art museum. His eyes grew large and wild as he encountered two paintings by Gauguin. He stood in silence before them, and then let out a loud grunt of dissatisfaction.

"You... you!" he growled, and moved on.

Not five steps away, he froze in his tracks. A wall filled with Van Goghs! *Mine! Mine!* He could not understand what his paintings were doing away from his home studio. He grabbed at the first one and began to remove it. An alarm sounded instantly, and just as quickly a guard seized his arms.

"These are mine! I want them back! Why do you have my paintings?" bellowed Nicholas, attempting to free himself.

Within seconds he was hustled off to a small room and handcuffed. There he sat alone until the police appeared to take him to the county jail.

"Why are you doing this to me? All I want is what's mine."

"Oh, those Van Goghs were yours, mister?" inquired the officer, escorting him to a waiting car.

"Yes, I painted them!"

"Ah, so you're the great painter himself, eh?"

"Yes… yes, I am *the* great painter," replied Nicholas, indignantly.

An assessment of Nicholas' mental health concluded he was highly delusional and a potential danger to himself, if not others. While his parents were loath to do so, they agreed to place him under close psychiatric care, which ultimately lasted for the remainder of his life. At the Saint-Paul Center, only 12 miles from the Wacker's home, Nicholas was allowed to continue to pursue his life's singular passion. As the months and then years passed, Anna and Ted visited their son every Friday without fail. They would sit patiently and watch as he produced his newest Van Gogh painting. When the number of canvasses began to overrun his room, they stored them in his former room at home.

And there things stood for 15 years. One day, the art critic who had taken Nicholas' work to task at his first and only gallery exhibit contacted the Wackers. His curiosity over the fate of the young wannabe had surfaced when Woodley had stumbled over his review while putting together a collection of his musings for a planned book. The Wackers told him of their son's sad existence, revealing how he continued to replicate Van Gogh's art. This fascinated the critic, who asked to see what Nicholas had done in the many years since his negative critique.

The Wackers agreed, and Woodley spent the afternoon closely examining what were now hundreds of canvasses in Nicholas' old bedroom. He was astounded by what he saw. Not only was the institutionalized artist prolific, but the quality of his replications was astonishing.

"May I take some of these to show my colleagues at the university? I really think they're quite extraordinary, even if they are copies of Van Gogh's paintings," asked Woodley.

The Wackers agreed and then waited to hear back from Woodley, hoping their son's lifelong efforts would be recognized as exceptional even if they were copies.

Two weeks later, while visiting Nicholas, he announced that the painting he was just then completing was Van Gogh's last oil. It was unusual though similar to the last batch Nicholas had painted since they'd seen him. While the canvasses were consistent with Van Gogh's style, the subject matter was very different. Several canvasses contained scenes of planets and strange floating machines.

"What are those, Nicholas? I don't think Van Gogh ever painted such things," said Anna.

"These were paintings that he never showed anyone. He kept them out of sight, and then they were lost."

Nicholas' referral to Van Gogh in the third person surprised and startled the Wackers, since their son had not spoken in his own voice since his breakdown. Nor had he acknowledge them as his parents during this period.

"I'm done," declared Nicholas. "I want to go home."

The Wackers could not contain their emotions and quickly informed their son's overseers of his obvious breakthrough. A week later they returned to the Gifford Center to pick up their miraculously restored son.

As soon as they arrived at the institution, they were informed that Nicholas had gone missing that morning and that a search for him was underway. The State Police had been called in and the Wackers joined in the search. After two days, Nicholas remained missing, and his parents returned home to await further word. The next day they were told the body of their 37 year-old son was found in an adjacent wheat field. It appeared he had died from a self-inflicted wound.

Their deep grief was interrupted a week after their son's funeral by a call from James Woodley.

"I'm so very sorry for your loss. Nicholas was an amazing individual. More amazing than I ever thought, I must admit. I have some news about your son's paintings. May I come by later? I think you'll want to know what I have to tell you."

When Anna answered the doorbell a half-hour later, she hardly recognized Woodley, because of the strange expression on his face.

"Thank you for letting me come right over. I wanted you to hear this from me before it gets out to the media."

"Media? What do you mean?" asked Ted, inviting Woodley inside.

"Well... " the art critic took a deep breath. "Several prominent art historians have evaluated your son's paintings, and they have concluded that there are no inconsistencies between those of Van Goghs's and Nicholas'. Indeed, they could not prove that they were *not* originals, although the originals are hanging in museums throughout the world. At first they even considered that those in the museums might be forgeries and that your son had somehow acquired the originals. That hypothesis was soon discounted as totally impossible and ridiculous."

The Wackers were stunned and confused by the news. For several moments they attempted to speak, but their voices had abandoned them. Finally, Ted was able to squeeze out a few words. "What are you saying? We know he painted them. We saw him do it time and time again. That's all he ever did. It was his life."

"I don't know what to tell you. It does seem way beyond coincidental. We're really all blown away by this. But there's more."

"What do you mean?' asked Anna, in a barely discernible whisper.

Woodley hesitated as if trying himself to grasp the meaning of what he was about to say. Well, *ah...* the experts ran a test on the oils Nicholas used in his paintings... "

"And?"

"They determined they were at least *120* years old," muttered Woodley, fixing his gaze on a family photograph of Nicholas as a child. *The eyes*, he thought. *Just look at those eyes.*

Perpetuity

Eternity is in love with itself.

~ Anonymous

Seth Perkins was about to turn 170 years old but looked like a man in his 50s. He was one of the first so-called Perpetuals. Only a decade ago it had been discovered that one percent of the world's population ceased to age beyond what was then considered midlife. Every country had Perpetuals, and the World Census Bureau calculated that the U.S. alone had 3.5 million of them. Because of their extraordinary attribute, they were regarded with both awe and envy.

The medical and science communities had yet to determine why 70 million humans escaped the curse of mortality and the wrath that accompanied it. Religious communities had various theories about the eternality of Perpetuals. Some sects saw it as the work of the devil and treated them with contempt and suspicion, while others attributed it to an act of their God, believing that Perpetuals were imbued with special grace and purpose. Exactly what that was, naturally, inspired considerable speculation. For example, Jews held that they were the second incarnation of the Chosen People intended to ensure their tribe's imperishability. Meanwhile, Muslims argued that Perpetuals had been selected by their Prophet to lead the world's conversion to Islam. And so on…

These diverse views complicated life for many Perpetuals, most of whom were not believers in any particular form of worship, nor were they specific to any race, gender, or ethnicity. Gerontologists had concluded that the extraordinary longevity of Perpetuals was not inherited, although many families reported having two or more among their flock. As far as Seth could determine, he alone of his family possessed the remarkable trait after extensively probing the Perkins' ancestral history.

Like most Perpetuals, Seth had some misgivings about his status. But as far as he was concerned, the prospect of living forever outweighed any downsides to it. Several financial ventures had made him wealthy, and he was now into a happy third marriage. He had outlived his two previous wives. Although he had tried to hook up with a fellow Perpetual, things had never worked out. Thus, his current wife, Celia, was a mortal as well. She had only been 31 when he married her. Now she was closing in on 60, and Seth could recognize the telltale signs of physical deterioration that befell all non-Perpetuals. However, unlike with his other wives, he did not consider his current spouse's aging a turnoff. His deep love for her made it possible for him to look beyond it.

Seth had regretted not having children with his previous wives. In his thirties it had become apparent to him that he could not produce offspring. It would have been a comfort for him to have children and grandchildren as he piled on the years, but in that respect he was not alone. Reproduction was not possible for Perpetuals, a factor that remained as much a mystery as their agelessness.

Rather than weaken his bond with his third wife, his infertility strengthened it. He was her world and she was his, and he was determined to further their time together. However, he knew mortals came with an expiration date, although the average lifespan had increased significantly in the last few decades. Reaching one hundred was not so exceptional any longer, and more and more people were reaching 110. The eldest known non-Perpetual on record had been a Chilean woman who had finally expired at 128.

If I can have another 60 or 70 years with Celia, I will be eternally thankful, thought Seth, who was hopeful medical science would continue to have success extending human life. *Just let me be with her as long as possible.* Every day with his greatest love was better than the previous one. Because of the many exquisite moments he'd had with Celia, life had never been so sweet. His time with her had been the greatest of his nearly two centuries on the planet.

During the next two decades, Celia had managed to ward off the effects of aging remarkably well. But as she approached 80, her health took a sudden turn, and she was diagnosed with severe osteoporosis, which caused her to hunch over. It spoiled her perfect posture, detracting from her hourglass figure. It broke Seth's heart to see his wife suffering the ravages of advancing years, and it reminded him of her mortality.

"You are still young and will be forever, and I'm an old lady. You should find a young woman who can give you what you need," declared Celia.

"No one can give me what you can, darling. You have my heart and always will," replied Seth, feeling his world begin to crumble.

"But look at us. I could be your mother. How can you love a sickly old woman?"

Seth was aware how it looked to everyone, but his heart remained as deeply attached to Celia as it had at the start of their relationship. He could look beyond her faded beauty but not her suffering. Her pain became his pain. Seth remained at his wife's side as her ailments worsened, and his steadfastness earned him the admiration of all who knew Celia. But the end came with her death at age 84. It was decades earlier than Seth had hoped.

In the dark days that followed, Seth was beyond consolation. Life had lost its sweetness and meaning to him, and the prospect of living forever now turned into something burdensome and unappealing. His state of mind remained bleak as Celia's casket was lowered into the ground and no less so when he returned to the house he had shared with his deceased sweetheart.

Despite his hope that he might escape his angst in sleep, Seth found he could not escape his grief and achieve the oblivion he sought. He sat on the edge of the bed that he had shared with Celia and recalled their great love affair. However, as the night deepened, there was an inexplicable but very welcome change in his mood. His despair began to fade and soon was replaced by a feeling of indifference. *Is this something unique to my kind?* he wondered. *Can we just stop feeling sorrow? Is that, too, a part of who we are? What we are?*

46

Indeed, by dawn, all the grief he had felt over the loss of his beloved Celia was completely gone, supplanted by a sense of elation over the limitless prospects that lay ahead for him.

What the hell, I'm a Perpetual. There will be other Celias... so many other Celias, he thought, feeling as happy as he had ever felt.

He slept deeply, and in his dreams he beheld the countless wives he would one day love... and then *cease* to love.

If Things Were Made to Last Forever

There's nothing new to buy, said Jill.

And not a single thing to fix, Jack said.

I'm so bored with it all, said Jill.

Everything is so pristine, Jack said.

Like the day we bought it, said Jill.

What will we do today? Jack asked.

There's no reason to go to the mall, said Jill.

And nothing to get online, Jack said.

Everything still looks so good, said Jill.

Yeah, and it all works just fine, Jack said.

It's really a shame that things don't wear out, said Jill.

It was a better time when thing broke down, Jack said.

Those were the good old days, said Jill.

There was so much to do back then, Jack said.

And so many more places to go, said Jill.

I just wish things got old again, Jack said.

At least we do, said Jill.

Impact

There is no armour against fate.
~ James Shirley

Gus Harrington was reading the newspaper at his kitchen table and sipping his first coffee of the morning when a statement on CNN caught his attention: "The asteroid is now said to be on a collision course with Earth. It was expected to come within 50 thousand miles of the planet, but last night the Crimean Astrophysical Observatory has recalculated its path and discovered it is now headed directly toward us."

Gus stood and moved closer to the wall-mounted flat screen. "*What the…?*"

"The asteroid is calculated to be three-quarters of a mile wide. Experts say that any direct hit on Earth would possess the equivalent of a 750-kiloton bomb, enough to create massive destruction to the planet."

"Oh my God!" muttered Gus.

"Called Balave-1453MV135, the asteroid is expected to reach the planet in another 14 months and three days. Astrophysicists are attempting to determine just where the asteroid will touch down and the extent of damage the impact will cause."

Gus was not aware that his wife had been standing behind him and watching the report.

"Is it going to destroy everything? Are we all going to die?"

Her voice made him jump.

"Jesus, Cheryl! Don't do that!"

"What?"

"Sneak up on me. You scared me to death!" The expression of apprehension on his wife's face brought him back to the reality of the moment. "Sorry, honey, they don't know where it's going to hit. They're trying to figure that out now."

"I'm going to get Clare from school," said Cheryl, abruptly.

"Why? Nothing's going to happen. Not for 14 months anyway."

"I just want to hold her. We're probably all going to die," sniffled Cheryl, throwing her jacket on.

"Not necessarily. Maybe they'll shoot it out of the sky with a missile. They can do that, I've heard. Remember that movie?"

"And if they can't?" Cheryl grabbed her car keys from the counter and dashed from the house before Gus could say anything further.

Yeah, what if they can't? he thought, watching his wife pull out of the driveway and knocking over the recycling container in the process. *This can't be happening. It has to be a nightmare. Wake up, Gus... wake up.*

He had always wondered if the day would come when something from space would come tumbling down on Earth, threatening to abolish life on the planet. It had always seemed possible, if not probable, to him. Astronomers had claimed they had discovered more than 10,000 Near-Earth objects, as they called them, and that 1455 of them were classified as "potentially hazardous." *Jesus, that's a 14 percent chance of being hit,* calculated Gus.

"'This is not a Flyby," said a voice on the television.

A CNN reporter was now interviewing an expert on asteroids: "From what we know now, it appears that this object will hit Earth and cause extreme damage. Will it end life on Earth, as we know it? Probably not, but its likely impact is currently being assessed. We've recalculated its arrival and now project it to strike us on August 18th."

August 18th? That's only seven months away. They said 14 months. Now it's half that? Why can't they pin it down? Next, they're going to tell us it's hitting in three months...

"It is our estimate the asteroid strike will possess energy seven million times greater than the bomb dropped on Hiroshima."

We're all dead! One big flash of light: obliterated! Seven million times bigger? Fuck! How could anything survive?

"This doesn't necessarily mean that human and animal life will end, but..."

But? No but! We're all screwed! thought Gus.

The reporter suddenly interrupted the scientist, deferring to an incoming feed from the White House, where a press conference was about to start.

Gus sat at the kitchen table attempting to wrap his mind around what was happening. He looked out the window at the baby blue sky. *Incoming,* he thought. *Duck and cover. Shit! In the end, not a whimper but a bang, right? A big frigging bang!* He turned back to the television to find the president about to speak:

"My fellow Americans, as I speak to you, the leaders of nations around the globe are informing their citizens about the potential calamity that we all face from space. We are now planning a joint effort to strike the asteroid with several missiles carrying massive nuclear payloads. There is reasonable hope in the scientific community that this will divert the asteroid's current trajectory away from Earth. It is important not to panic in the face of this situation. Life must continue as normal while the efforts are undertaken to remove this threat."

No freaking way we're going to blow that huge bastard off its current path, Gus thought, suddenly feeling an overwhelming urge to heed the call of nature. And as he sat on the porcelain throne, his thoughts were racing. *Once we know when it's going to hit, we'll head in the opposite direction. Maybe find a cave. We'll need supplies. Load up on food right away before the store shelves are empty. Canned goods… water. Don't forget a can opener. Should I get a gun? Yeah, it'll get crazy out there. Oh, Jesus!*

Gus went to the garage to figure out what else might be useful for their survival. He gathered a box of items that included an ax and various tools, as well as battery powered hurricane lanterns and first aid kit. He then unloaded junk from the hatchback section of his SUV to make room for other necessary supplies for his family's escape. As he was checking his car's fluids and tires, the phone rang. It was the police.

"Mr. Harrington?"

"Yes."

"We have your wife in custody."

"What?"

"The principal of your daughter's elementary school reported she was ranting something about the end of the world. She got everyone spooked. They thought she was having some kind of psychotic episode and feared she might be a danger to students and staff."

"Yes, she was terribly upset when she heard the news of the asteroid. I'll be right there?"

"Oh, that…"

Before the voice at the other end of the receiver could continue, Gus hung up. He climbed into his car and drove to the police headquarters. A desk sergeant greeted him.

"I'm Gus Harrington. My wife is being held for causing a scene about the asteroid at my daughter's school?"

"Yeah, we had a number of incidents related to the CNN hacking."

"Hacking?"

"Some anarchist group cut into the regular broadcast with their own video that looked exactly like CNN's. They gave the false report about the asteroid hitting the planet. Had everyone totally convinced the end was coming."

"You're kidding."

"They knew what they were doing… that's for damn sure. Looked authentic."

"But the President was speaking!"

"Some impersonator had dubbed voice over the footage of the President that was taken at a previous news conference. Sounded exactly like him, though if you were paying close attention you could see he was saying other words. Still, these guys were good. That's what's so scary. Not easy to pull off something like they did."

"Man, were we duped. Never doubted the report for a second. Can I get my wife? Does she know the whole thing was a hoax?"

"Yeah, we told her. Took some convincing. Now she feels embarrassed about what happened at the school."

"Are there any charges?"

"No, it was all a misunderstanding. We had other people going goofy, too. Had to haul in about ten other folks who were going over the edge after seeing the bogus report on CNN."

The desk sergeant fetched Gus's wife, and they left the station.

"We'll pick up Clare at school, okay?" said Gus.

"I'm not going in. I feel so stupid and humiliated," replied Cheryl, with a hangdog expression.

When their daughter climbed into the car, she immediately asked her mother a question that compounded her dark mood.

"Are you crazy, mommy? They said you were at school."

"No, honey. Mommy was just upset because she thought something bad was going to happen to us," explained Cheryl.

"Is something bad going to happen to us?"

"No, nothing bad is going to happen to us." When Gus turned to give his daughter a reassuring smile, he missed the red light and drove into the intersection as a truck was speeding through it. Upon impact, the Harrington's car was engulfed in an unearthly flash of light.

When She was Gone

What is the worst of woes that wait an age?
What stamps the wrinkle deeper on the brow?
To view each loved one blotted from life's page,
And be alone on Earth, as I am now.
~ Lord Byron

Lois Dabney was always the life of the party, the focal point of any space she occupied… and then she died. It left her grieving husband, Bernie, reevaluating his life. He had depended on his spouse for the social activity the two enjoyed. She had been the one who had planned their outings and arranged get-togethers with friends. It was not something Bernie exceled at. His wife's gregarious nature had been one of the qualities that had most attracted him when they had first met in business school. He had always been awkward around people, an introvert, and it had been a fortunate act of fate that connected them. As soon as Lois sat at the desk next to him in that macroeconomics course, she was all he could think about. He was totally and irrevocably smitten.

Yet it took Bernie several classes before he had an exchange with Lois, and it was not an auspicious start to their relationship. He had spilled coffee on her as he turned away from the vending machine during a break in their class. Fortunately, the hot liquid had not hit her skin. However, Bernie showed such extreme concern it made Lois chuckle.

"I'm fine. Just a little on my skirt. No big damage, really," she assured her distraught classmate.

"So you're not burned? I'm such a klutz," apologized Bernie. "I'll pay to have it cleaned. It was completely my fault."

"It'll come out in the wash. I'll 'Shout it out.'"

Bernie's deadpan reaction to her attempt at humor caught Lois off guard.

"You know, the spot remover… Shout? *Shout* it out… ?"

After a pause, it dawned on Bernie that she was trying to make light of the situation, and he attempted a riposte of his own. "If that doesn't work, you can... ah, *scream* at it."

The lameness of his joke had the same affect on Lois as hers had on him. Bernie immediately realized how dumb his comeback sounded. After another short pause, Lois broke out laughing, and Bernie thought it was in reaction to his pathetic attempt at a rejoinder. When her chuckle turned into a sweet smile, he knew she wasn't mocking him.

"I'm Lois Miller. What year are you in?"

"Huh?" replied Bernie, lost in her large brown eyes. "Oh, I'm a junior in Accounting."

"I'm a junior, too... in Retailing. I'd like to own my own store someday."

"Really? That's... uh, ambitious. My goal is to work for a big accounting firm."

"Well, that's pretty ambitious, too. So your name is Bernie, right?"

"It is, but how do you know?"

"I heard the professor say your name once. You had the answer to the question nobody else did. I was really impressed."

"You were?"

"Yeah, I thought you were pretty smart, too."

Bernie could not keep from blushing, which returned the sweet smile to Lois's face.

"Guess we better get back to class," said Bernie, checking his watch.

Two more classes took place before Lois and Bernie spoke again, and it was Lois who initiated the conversation.

"There's a picnic sponsored by the retailing department this Sunday. Want to go? It'll be fun."

"I really don't know anybody in your major," demurred Bernie."

"You know me, and I'll introduce you to my friends. Come on."

Bernie was thrilled that Lois had asked him to the event but as usual was uncomfortable with the prospect of a having to function in a social setting. All his life, he had tried to avoid group activities, but his attraction to Lois was stronger than his aversion to dealing with strangers. To his great relief and satisfaction, being with Lois made the experience much more bearable than he could ever have imagined. It was that way for the entire 31 years with her.

In the weeks following Lois's funeral, Bernie stuck close to home, only occasionally venturing out to a dinner party held by the friends he had shared with his wife. At these gatherings, he had little to offer. Without his spouse by his side encouraging him to join in the dialog, he remained mostly silent. Gradually, the invitations became fewer and fewer. This did not upset Bernie at first, but as weeks turned into months, he began to feel almost shunned by those with whom he and Lois had spent considerable time.

Before long, he wasn't hearing from anyone, and a deep loneliness filled his days and nights, especially the latter. Even people in his workplace seemed to ignore him more than usual. The one person he regarded as a true friend, Mel Colby, was on a work project in Germany, so they could only exchange emails. And that did little to mitigate his growing sense of aloneness. He longed for his friend's return, and counted the days that separated them.

He and Mel had clicked quickly on first meeting, principally because of Mel's outgoing, if not flamboyant, personality. For reasons Bernie had yet to really fathom, Mel had taken a strong liking to him. He speculated that it might be because he provided Mel with a perfect audience for his steady stream of jokes and comments about their fellow workers and life in general. Bernie also thought it could have to do with the fact that Mel was a bachelor and therefore in need of a steady friend. Whatever it was, Bernie was thrilled to have Mel's attention. In fact, his fondness for Mel was only rivaled by his profound feelings for Lois, who liked his friend as well.

"He's really such an interesting person, and so funny. It's nice that you two get along so well," Bernie recalled Lois saying, on more than one occasion.

On the Monday Colby was to return to work stateside, Bernie felt better than he had for months. He looked forward to reconnecting with the only male with whom he had ever felt so close a friendship. In fact, his affection for Colby had been greater than that for his own brother, who he had not seen in years because of an old feud over their parents' will.

As soon as Bernie spotted Colby exiting the elevator, he ran to greet him. "Mel!"

"Hey, Bernie. Good to see you, buddy. You look like you've lost a lot of weight."

"A few pounds. I needed to anyway."

"Don't we all. Look, I've been wanting to tell you in person how bad I feel about Lois passing on. What a loss. She was a great lady. I'm sure you miss her terribly. I do, too. We all do."

"Thanks, Mel." As the two men walked down the corridor, the ring on Colby's pinky finger caught Bernie's eye. *That looks familiar*, thought Bernie, and then he realized it was the ring Lois had given to him on their tenth anniversary. "Can I see your hand, Mel? Your left hand."

"Huh? Why?"

Bernie grabbed Colby's hand and inspected the ring. "That's *my* ring. How did you . . .? Why are you wearing it?"

"What do mean?" replied Colby, pulling his hand away and burying it in his pocket.

"Lois gave that to me when we were on vacation in Wyoming twenty years ago. It's Indian turquoise. I thought I had lost it. Didn't dare tell Lois I had."

"Come on, Bernie. There are lots of rings like this one. Why would it be yours?"

"Why don't you tell me, Mel? Yeah... why, indeed, would it be mine?"

"Let's talk later. We have a lot to catch up on. Beers at Wheeler's after work, okay? Calm down, too. You're making something out of nothing, pal... really."

Colby disappeared into his office, leaving Bernie alone to ponder what had just happened. *It is my ring. Handmade by a Ute. None like it. One of a kind. What's he doing with it? Why does he have it on?*

Bernie decided to make a quick run home to make absolutely certain the ring was gone. *I looked for it everywhere... everywhere. I know it's not there,* thought Bernie, climbing into his car.

Hours later he knew he was right. The ring was nowhere to be found. He scanned every inch of his bedroom and home office, but came up empty. *Bullshit. The ring is gone, and Colby has it. But how...?*

Back at the office, Bernie tried to locate Colby, but he was not to be found. Finally the workday ended, and Bernie headed to Wheeler's Sports Pub to meet up with him. An anxious hour passed, and only then did he spot Colby entering the bar.

"Hey, guy, sorry I'm late. Had an all day meeting with clients at their shop in Natick." As Colby took a seat, Bernie noticed he was no longer wearing the ring.

"Why'd you take it off?"

"What?" replied Colby, eyeing Bernie warily.

"The ring you were wearing this morning... *my* ring."

"Oh, I took it off to wash my hands. Just didn't put it back on."

"Let me see it."

"I left it back in my office."

"Why'd you do that?"

"Look, you're getting all upset over nothing. I got that ring through a catalog. You know, the Sundance flier you get in the mail? I liked it and ordered it a couple years ago."

"I never saw it before."

"Just started wearing it."

"Did Lois give it to you?"

Sitting alone in the bar before Colby arrived, the thought had occurred to Bernie that his wife might have given the ring to Colby since he had only worn it in the weeks after she had given it to him. *That's not something she would do... is it? Was there something going on? Were they having... ?* "You were having an affair with Lois, weren't you?" blurted Bernie, surprised at his own words.

"Whoa, Bernie! What the hell are you saying? Me and Lois? That's ridiculous. Surely you're kidding, right?"

Bernie weighed Colby's reaction and probed his expression. *He's lying. The bastard is lying. How could he do this? My best friend. My only friend.* "Okay, look Bernie... Lois and I became good friends, and she gave me the ring as a symbolic gesture of our companionship. She said you never wore it, so she wanted me to have it. Said it sealed our friendship. I didn't wear it in case you noticed it. In fact, I was going to give it back to Lois, but then I went to Germany for six months. Then she died. I put it on in her honor, and then I forgot I was wearing it this morning. Jet lag, you know. Not thinking clearly."

"So she gave my tenth anniversary gift to you? Well, I think she was more than just a good *friend* of yours, Mel."

"*You're* a good *friend* of mine, Bernie. Why would... ?"

"Exactly, why would you?"

Bernie rose abruptly and left the bar, returning to his empty house. There he paced about, wondering what course of action he should take. *First I lose my wife and then I learn this. I've lost everything,* mused Bernie, opening a metal box and removing a pistol from it. *I can't deal with this. It's just too much. I have no one anymore. I have to do something.*

Bernie sat in his backyard and watched as the sky turned dark. *I can't let this happen. I won't,* he mumbled. He then got into his car and drove to Colby's condo. The second time he pressed the bell, Colby opened the door, and Bernie pressed the gun into his side.

"What's going on, Bernie? Jesus, you're acting crazy. Is that loaded?"

"Sit down, Mel. I have to ask you something."

"Please don't shoot. The thing with Lois just happened. We didn't mean to get involved. Really, you have to believe me. She loved you, and you were... *are*, my best friend. Don't do this, Bernie."

"I have to. Get on your knees, Mel."

"What? No, no, don't... "

"Get on your knees... *NOW!*"

"Okay... okay," Colby whimpered.

"I got to do this, man. It's the only way."

"Why?" Why do you have to do this?" asked Colby, beginning to sob.

"Because it's the only way I can go on. Now, repeat after me... "

"PLEASE, no!" pleaded Colby, his arms outstretched toward Bernie.

"Repeat after me, Mel. 'I will remain Bernie's friend forever.'"

"Huh?"

"Say it! 'I will remain Bernie's friend forever.'"

"Okay, yes, 'I will remain Bernie's friend forever.'"

"Again."

"I will remain Bernie's friend *forever*.'"

"You mean it?"

"Totally! Absolutely! Friends forever!"

"Okay," said Bernie, putting the gun down.

Life Insurance

Oh, dry the starting tear, for they were heavily insured.
~ W.S. Gilbert

Following a mild coronary episode, Mark Duress decided he should review his life insurance policy. The day he returned home from a 48-hour stay in the hospital, he searched for it, but without success.

"Why don't you just call the insurance company and have them mail it?" suggested Kelli, his wife of 25 years.

"Snail mail takes too long. I'll just drop by their office and have them make a copy and maybe go over it with me. Want to make sure everything's in order."

"In order? You're fine, Mark. The doctor said it was nothing chronic. Don't get all fatalistic because you had a little heart fart."

"I'm not. I actually have no memory of what the policy looks like. It's smart to know what you're paying for and if you can get more for your dollar."

So Mark made an appointment with Furlong Indemnity for the next day, and arrived at the designated time. The company that held his insurance policy had changed its ownership and location a couple of times and was now housed on the third floor of what looked like a new building with a faux gothic facade. When he entered its lobby, he discovered the elevator was out of order, so he reluctantly took the stairs. *Shouldn't be exerting myself like this after the heart episode,* he thought, moving slowly and deliberately up the cement steps.

"May I help you, sir?" asked a doleful-looking receptionist when he entered the insurance office.

"I have a 1:15 appointment with Mr. Carson."

"Oh, you must be Mr. Duress."

Mark nodded, "That would be me."

"I'll let Walter know you're here. Please have a seat. There's a new *People Magazine* in the rack right over there, if you'd like to read something."

Mark thanked the woman and took a seat, ignoring the reading material. Before he had a chance to settle in, the receptionist instructed him to go to the end of the corridor and take a right to the second door.

"Walter is waiting for you, Mr. Duress."

"Thank you." About six steps down the hallway, Mark was stopped in his tracks by a painting hanging on the beige-colored wall. *What the hell is that?* he wondered, moving closer to what was a depiction of a burned-out house with two sheet-covered bodies on the ground before it. *Why the hell would they display such an awful picture? Who would paint such an atrocity?*

As he continued down the dimly-lit hall, he encountered yet another painting—one even more grotesque than the first. *Christ!* he gulped at the sight of it, his stomach churning. The images were repellent, to say the least. Two wrecked vehicles blocked a highway. A bloodied body lay across the mangled hood of one car, having obviously been launched through its windshield. Next to the twisted wrecks lay three other mortally wounded accident victims. *What the... ? This is unbelievable!*

He turned away, feeling nauseous, only to spy another painting that portrayed a flooded street with several corpses floating in the murky water. *Too much! I've had it*, he thought, deciding to leave the insurance office.

"Mr. Duress?" came a voice from behind him.

Mark swung around and found himself a few steps from a tall, gaunt figure in a black three-piece suit.

"I'm Walt Carson. Please, come into my office. It's good to see you."

For a moment, Mark considered leaving, but then turned and followed Carson.

"Have a seat. I don't believe we've actually met in the flesh, although I am familiar with your policy."

The agent's exceptionally ornate desk looked as if it were on loan from Versailles, thought Mark.

"Beauty, isn't it? Got it at an estate sale. A client. Sadly, she came to a tragic end. Had plenty of coverage, as you might imagine for someone owning this treasure. Speaking of coverage, that's why you're here. To make sure your loved ones are taken care of in the event of your untimely absence." Carson smiled broadly, revealing a row of uneven and discolored teeth.

"I just want to make certain everything is where it should be. I think it probably is."

"Well, not really, Mr. Duress. May I call you Mark?"

"Yes, that's what my mother called me," replied Mark, attempting to lighten the oppressive atmosphere.

"Thank you, *Mark*. Actually, your coverage is less than it should be, and I think that places you in duress. Oh, I'm sorry. I didn't mean to make a joke about your last name."

"No insult taken," answered Mark. "It's pronounced 'Dures,' though. No extra syllable or emphasis on the 'ess.'"

"Oh, please excuse me. I've been pronouncing it wrong all along. Anyway, your policy really could use upgrading . . ."

As Carson spoke, Mark found that he could not shake the horrific images adorning the hallway. "Excuse me. May I ask why you have those shocking paintings hanging out there? They're really... well, *hideous*."

"Au contraire, Mark. They're quite heartrending," objected Carson, his expression assuming an air of superiority.

"Huh?"

"They're depictions of clients who lacked sufficient life insurance... "

"That's, ah ... "

"Touching?"

"No! ghoulish. Who would paint such things?"

Carson's expression darkened. "A talented artist, I would say. Now, back to the point I was trying to make. You should consider increasing your coverage substantially, Mr. *Duress*."

"Substantially? No, I can't afford to do that. In fact, I'll probably leave it the way it is, Mr. *Carson.*"

"That would be unwise."

"Look, I really came here only to get a copy of my policy," said Mark, looking at his watch. "Can I have that copy, please? I've got to be going."

"Again, let me advise you to increase your numbers. You never know when something fateful may occur, and right now you are not adequately covered to provide adequate support for your family... should something unexpected happen to you."

"I'll think about it. Goodbye, Mr. Carson."

"Goodbye, indeed, Mr. *Duress,*" hissed the insurance agent.

"Why the tone? What are you suggesting?"

"Only that you should get more *protection.*"

Mark gave Carson a disgusted look and left his office. He moved quickly down the hall, feeling a compelling desire to be away from the premises. He avoided looking at the disturbing artwork as he moved to the end of the corridor. Just before the receptionist's area, he came to a sudden halt. A painting he had not seen before leapt out at him. *Huh? No, this can't be real...* he thought, as he stood before the worst of all of the hall's grotesqueries. *It's... it's me!*

The canvas possessed a clear likeness of him in a heap at the bottom of a staircase. It was apparent that he had fallen and snapped his neck. The very sight of the grim image provoked him. "Son of a bitch! How could he... ?"

Mark pulled the painting from the wall and marched back to Carson's office. He pushed the door open and entered what seemed like the darkest corner of night. Before he could say a word, however, the room was flooded with light. Mark regained his purpose just as quickly.

"What is this, Mr. Carson? Who do you... ?"

As he addressed the back of Carson's office chair, the agent swiveled around and faced him. "What seems to be the problem, Mr. Duress?"

"Look at this," shouted Mark, holding the painting in front of Carson.

"So? What's your point?"

"The goddamn painting is of me with a broken neck!"

"What are you talking about?"

Mark turned the painting toward himself.

"This is what I... "

"Yes, Mr. Duress? You were saying?"

Mark was speechless. The canvas was blank. "But there was a picture of me dead. My face was blue. I must have fallen down some stairs."

Carson smiled, and his expression filled Mark with an overwhelming sense of foreboding. "As I said, you never know when things are going to take a bad turn. Perhaps you've reconsidered increasing the amount of your life insurance policy?"

"Yes... *yes, I have!*" answered Mark, without a moment's hesitation.

"Good, I thought you would see the light, so to speak. Here's a copy of your upgraded policy," said Carson, with a forced smile.

Mark left the office quickly, feeling apprehensive and confused. On his way out, he tried to avoid looking at the grisly paintings lining the walls, but only partially succeeded. As he reached the stairs preparing to descend them, he felt something cold push against his back.

The Shroud of Turn In

As I'm about to take a nap, I see a face in the quilt. It reminds me of a 1930s actor who played a tough guy in gangster movies. He had a bulbous nose and ruddy cheeks. The bed cover is an old family heirloom, so I think the face might belong to a relative it once covered. Maybe it's a dead ancestor come to haunt my dreams. But I don't think it's that, though. Its expression is not menacing. In fact, it makes me smile, and after a while I like that it's there next to me. Eventually, I talk to it before I doze off. It doesn't respond at first, but then it does. What it says upsets me. *Shut up! I'm trying to sleep!* "I'm only trying to be your friend," I say.

Septic Children

It must be said that charity can, in no way, exist
along with mortal sin.
~ Thomas Aquinas

Hello there. Name's Johnny McKenna, and I'd like to ask you a question. That is, if you don't mind. Thank you.

First, allow me to tell you a little about myself. Until I was nearly seven years old, I lived at St. Mary's on Dublin Road, in Tuam, Ireland. It was referred to as the "Home" by everyone, but it wasn't a home in the true sense of the word. It was more like a former military billet or an old mill that had been emptied of its crude tools and only slightly modified to accommodate a bunch of parentless kids and members of a religious order.

We were cared for by the Bon Secours nuns. I use the words "cared for" very loosely, because the treatment provided us was nearly always harsh and without compassion. Yes, the sisters watched over us but in a manner similar to that of a guard over his prisoners. The nuns showed us little affection and, in point of fact, appeared more burdened by and resentful of our presence than anything else.

To say we lived a meager existence is an understatement. We were fed twice a day–usually cold mush in the morning and boiled potatoes and bread for supper. Occasionally, we were given a shred of mutton, usually on a high holy day, like Christmas or Easter. The sisters would make us say an extra Hail Mary for receiving such a bounty.

Every child possessed only the clothes on his back, and on Saturday night we stripped naked so that our threadbare garments could be washed while we were sleeping. This created a particular problem for us, because the single blanket we were allotted was hardly enough to keep us from freezing on the bitter winter nights. So, as soon as the lights were turned off promptly at 7 o'clock, we would slip in bed with another child in order to generate enough warmth to lessen our individual misery. This was dangerous, since if we were caught cuddling together–and we often were–the nuns became very agitated and seized the opportunity to punish us.

"You filthy little urchins! What were you doing together in the same bed without a stitch on? Shameful! The apple doesn't fall far from the tree. For your penance, you'll spend the rest of the night in the hall until the breakfast bell."

We were told to kneel with our faces to the wall. As we did, we received a hard whack on our bare rumps with the sister's rosary beads. Soon the burning of our flesh gave way to a horrible numbness from the icy currents that flowed through the dark corridor. At dawn, our damp clothes were tossed to us, and we were informed that for being such disgusting creatures we would also be deprived of our breakfast.

It was during the coldest months that there was the most sickness at the Home. Practically every child had the sniffles and deep phlegmy hacks. Rather than inspiring sympathy in the nuns, it seemed to compound their general disdain for us. Without anything else to wipe our noses on, our shirtsleeves became hardened with the gooey contents of our oozing nostrils. When a nun caught someone wiping snot on his or her sleeve, the culprit would be duly cowed in the most egregious way.

"You're less than a pig's slop, child! Disgusting animal, you are! Take that shirt off, and you'll go without it until it is cleansed of your foulness!" bellowed Sister Meaghan, the nun we most feared because of her explosive temper.

No one incurred the wrath of the habited mucus monitors more than little Sean O'Halloran. And no one went without his pullover more than he did. Two years younger than me and barely up to my elbow, he seemed to be singled out more than anyone else by the ever-scowling brides of the Almighty. Because he was more vulnerable and helpless than the rest of us, I tried as best I could to keep him out of harm's way, but my efforts were seldom effective.

"There's no room in Heaven for a devil's child such as you, O'Halloran! The Lord keeps vulgar beings from entering His paradise so as not to contaminate it," barked Sister Meaghan, who appeared to gain distinct pleasure in berating Snotty Sean, as he came to be known.

Not long after he was christened with the sad moniker, his chest congestion worsened and he was removed from the sleeping hall and placed in the orphanage's tiny infirmary. The single bed that it contained was already occupied by another suffering soul, so Sean was given a makeshift place to recline on the floor. For two days I saw him curled up beneath a thin blanket as we passed the sick room on our way to and from our meals. On the third day, he was gone.

When I asked a nun where he was, I was told in no uncertain terms to mind my own business. It was the last we ever saw of poor Snotty Sean. That's the way it was with other children that got sick, too. They just went away... never to return. We all figured they'd either gone to the hospital or were adopted. Billy Morrissey, an older kid who swept floors in the infant ward, told us that the babies didn't last long before they were taken away.

"They wrap them up and bring them someplace else, especially the ones that got the croup bad. They never come back either. Maybe they died or got taken by somebody for adoption."

We all speculated about the fate of those no longer among us, and we tried to convince ourselves that they had either been taken in by loving families or transferred to a better facility with nicer sisters. Yet the thought that our fellow orphans may really have come to a bad end haunted many of us... and would forever. Although a wonderful couple from Galway eventually added me to their kindly household, I've carried the bleak experience of the Home with me to this day.

The mystery of what had happened to so many of the less fortunate at the orphanage was finally and shockingly solved. It turns out that hundreds of infants and small children at St. Mary's had been consigned to its septic tank after succumbing to illness or malnutrition. The dead were not even given a pauper's burial. With no regard for the fact that they had been human beings–if not God's children, the Sisters of Bon Secours saw fit to rid themselves of their deceased wards by dumping their remains into a stink hole on the grounds of the Home. This was done without ceremony or markers signifying the site of the remains.

I was having breakfast with my six-year-old grandson when I opened the *Irish Examiner* and was confronted by the following story: *Horrific discovery of hundreds of children buried in a septic tank at St. Mary's in Tuam in Galway...*

There it was... the answer to the question that had possessed me. I was overwhelmed with feelings of rage and sadness for all the Snotty Seans that were treated as if they were nothing more than toxic waste to be flushed from the planet by representatives of a so-called compassionate God.

Sorry, I... please give me a second to get the lump out of my throat. It's been there a very long time... So then, about that question I'd like to ask you:

Was there ever anything worse than the Mother Church of Ireland?

Things You Get When Your Parents Die

We pass through things temporal, that we finally
lose not the things eternal.
~ Prayer Book, 1662

Most of the sadness Leman Cummings felt about the recent passing of his parents had to do with how little they had to show for their existence on the planet. They left nothing of material value despite their years of hard toiling in the textile mills of Lawrence, Massachusetts. The elderly Cummingses had finally been forced to sell their modest house in order to pay for their care in a local nursing home.

Leman had been able to contribute very little to their upkeep, due to the low salary he was paid as a hand truck operator on the shipping and receiving platform at a large appliance store. The small amount he had managed to give them had all but emptied his savings account, and his efforts to seek a better paying job were thwarted by his lack of higher education. Although he had accumulated a significant number of credits, he remained three courses shy of receiving his associate degree in business from Northern Essex Community College.

What he possessed of his deceased parents estate consisted of one small file container, a faded photo album, a few dishes and pots that had seen better days, and two sets of worn sheets and blankets that had been in the family since he was a child. With the exception of a tired Naugahyde recliner and wobbly end table that Leman had added to his sparse collection, all of the Cummings' old furniture had been either discarded or taken by the Salvation Army. *Afraid they don't do much to improve on this crummy apartment*, thought Leman, surveying his stark surroundings.

He had moved from his parents' house three years earlier in an attempt to finally declare his independence and begin his own life as an adult. However, for a number of reasons, he had continued to spend at least as much time with his mother and father as he did in his drab accommodations. For one thing, his mother was a good cook, and he didn't like making his own meals. Secondly, he could keep a watch on their declining health, which, in the case of his father, was serious. And, as he had no real social life, being with his parents helped mitigate his loneliness.

Leman's relationship with a fellow worker, Cary Boswell, had gone sour after a year and a half, and since then he'd been in such a deepening funk about his life that he had actually contemplated suicide. The needs of his ailing parents had kept him from doing so, but in their absence the notion of ending his barren existence had reasserted itself. Now, as he sat in the gloom of his cheap apartment, he considered ways of taking his life.

Got no gun, so that's off the list. Death by asphyxiation? But how do you do that without a gas stove? Jump out the window. Only on the second floor though, so the best I'd do is break some bones and hurt like hell. Pills… yeah, pills are good. Just go to sleep, and it's over. Could take mom's old meds. Enough there to take down a wooly mammoth.

As Leman considered his options, he opened the metal file container that he had removed from his parents' house. He had casually scanned its contents before, but now he discovered a note addressed to him from his father. It both touched and depressed him.

Dear Son, I'm afraid our lives haven't amounted to much, but we've always tried our best to give you what we could. When you look at this ring, let it remind you that we loved you with all of our hearts. Dad (and Mom)

Ring? What ring? Leman wondered, digging through the box. Finally, he dumped everything it contained onto the floor. Amid the pile of papers, he spotted what he hoped was the ring. *There it is*, he mumbled, reaching for it and lifting it toward his eyes. The silver band contained a black stone with what looked like a tiny diamond at its center. *Was it Dad's? Never saw it before. Why didn't he ever wear it?*

He attempted to put it on his ring finger, but no matter how hard he pushed, he couldn't get it past his thick knuckle. *Dad had such small hands,* he recalled. The ring failed to fit his pinky as well, being too loose to wear without it slipping off. *Maybe I can get it sized to fit me,* thought Leman, placing it in his pants pocket. Later in the morning, he decided to take it to a jeweler to see if it could be adjusted to his finger's dimension. However, on his way to the mall, another idea occurred to him. *Maybe I could sell it. Could be worth something. Sure could use the money.* As soon as the thought entered his head, he chided himself for considering it. *It's your father's ring, Leman. His legacy to you. For God's sake, that wouldn't be right.*

Yet, the idea stuck and soon Leman found himself at a local pawnshop. *Let me just see what it brings,* he reasoned, entering the store.

"You wanna sell or pawn it?" asked the middle age man behind a display case filled with all manner of objects, including watches, bracelets, and rings.

"I don't know. What will you give me if I sell it?"

"It ain't very valuable. Onyx with a little diamond chip. Give you a hundred bucks, and that's more than I should. It's old, so that might make it worth a little more."

Leman thought about it for a moment. "Okay," he answered, surprised at himself for so readily opting for the money.

On his way home, he tried to fight off the rising guilt he felt for peddling what clearly had been a treasure to his father. By the time he reached his apartment, he felt sick about it. *I can't believe I did that. Sorry, Dad. Your son is such a loser.*

Leman sat in his apartment with the lights out, considering his shameless act and thinking about his parents and their many kindnesses to him. After less than an hour, he decided to return to the pawnshop and buy back the ring. *Whatever he wants, I'll give him what I can,* resolved Leman, turning the lamp on. As he rose from his father's tattered recliner, his eyes fell on a shiny object on the end table. *What the... can't be...* There before him was his father's ring. *How?* He picked it up, and carefully inspected it. *It's his ring, but that's impossible... !*

After his initial shock, Leman put the ring in his pocket and returned to the pawnshop.

"I found this in my apartment. I have no idea how it got there. I'm thinking I might have accidentally put it back into my pocket and took it," explained Leman, holding the ring before the pawnbroker.

"Huh? What are you talking about? I sold it right after you left. Some old guy came in and bought it. Paid two hundred bucks for it. How'd you get it?"

"What was his name?"

"Don't take no names."

"What did he look like?"

"I don't know. He was old, like I said. Had a mole on his chin and no uppers. You know, no teeth on top."

Leman shuddered at the description. His father had lost his upper plate a year before he died and had refused to replace it because of the cost. And he'd had a mole just like the one the pawnbroker described; it had always bothered Leman, who had long suggested his father get it removed in case it proved malignant. "Where did he go?"

"Through that door," replied the pawnbroker, looking at Leman with growing irritation.

"So you don't know anything else about the person who bought this ring?"

"I told you everything I know, buddy."

Leman left the pawnshop and returned to his apartment, all the while clutching the ring in his pocket. *How could this happen? Was it my father's ghost? That can't be. I'm losing it. Dad, what's going on?*

Once again, Leman sat in the darkness of his apartment and pondered the day's unsettling events. Eventually, he drifted off to sleep. In his dreams, his parents stood over his crib smiling at him lovingly, encouraged him as he attempted to ride his first two-wheeler, watched with pride as he performed in a school choir, cheered him on at a little league game...

When he awoke, he was filled with deep gratitude for everything they had provided him. "Thank you, Mom and Dad, for everything. And I'm really sorry for selling your ring, Dad," said Leman, reaching into his pocket for it. But it wasn't there. *Don't tell me I lost it!* He quickly reached for the light switch. When the room brightened, he noticed that his father's heirloom was now on his ring finger... and it fit perfectly.

Was

Everyone becomes a "was."
It's how we all end up.
Our forever and eternal status,
Just a memory to those we knew…
Jim was such a nice guy.
He was a real gentle person.
I think no one was as kind as Jim.
He certainly was there for me.
I was thinking of him the other day.
So was I, in fact.
It was so sad to see him pass.
Was that a year ago?
Hi Bill. How are you?
We were talking about old, sweet Jim.
Oh, him. He was such an ass!

What You Dread You Become

For as our diff'rent ages move,
'Tis so ordained, would Fate but mend it,
That I shall be past making love,
When she begins to comprehend it.

~ Matthew Prior

It was when Kyle's fiancé, Jill, rose from bed naked on one of their sleepy weekend mornings that he first realized how thin she had become. Why hadn't he noticed it before? Her shoulder blades were so pronounced they reminded him of the living skeletons in the Nazi concentration camps. He said nothing at first, but later in the day when he saw her gaunt figure bent over in the garden, he spoke up. He instantly regretted the tactlessness of his remark.

"My God, Jill, you look anorexic. Like Karen Carpenter."

"Gee… thanks for the compliment," she replied, continuing to claw at the soil.

"Sorry, I didn't mean that. It just came out. But, Jesus, honey, you're so skinny… too skinny.

"I haven't felt good the last few weeks."

"Few weeks? Why didn't you say something?"

"Because, I figured it wasn't anything. Maybe a low grade virus."

"What are your symptoms?"

"A little nauseous. Stomach aches and my back hurts sometimes."

"So you've decided bending over like that will help?"

"It feels okay today."

"Well, you should make a… "

"Doctor's appointment? I already have. Tomorrow afternoon. Can you take me?"

Two days after Jill's ultrasound, she and Kyle sat in the doctor's office. The news was devastating. Jill had one of the most lethal of all cancers—pancreatic.

"The good news is, we caught it early and it's the kind that we can operate on. Look, I'm not going to be coy about this. The mortality rate *is* high. But people *do* survive, and we're going to do whatever we can help you to be one of them."

Jill sat speechless, clutching Kyle's hand. An awkward silence was finally broken by a question from Kyle to the doctor. "When can we... ?"

"I'd like to set up the surgery for next week. Not smart to delay. The sooner we take it out, the better."

The word 'it' reminded Jill of the movie *Alien*. The wormy creature that had leaped from the ribcage of the astronaut was called an 'it." The thought activated Jill's vomit reflex, but she was able to quell the nearly overpowering urge to gush forth.

"Where?" asked Kyle.

"Brighton General downtown. I've conferred with Doctor Carlyle, the oncologist. He'll be handling your surgery and recovery. He's outstanding. One of the best in the field."

Jill gave out a whimper and then took a deep breath. "Okay... okay, I can do this."

"Of course you can. And I'm optimistic about the outcome. We all need to hold on to a positive frame of mind during this challenging time. You're young and can have a good long life, but some things require you fight."

Fight of her life, thought Kyle, his strong sense of fatalism kicking in. *She probably won't make it. God almighty... I surely won't make it if she doesn't.*

On the trip home, Kyle suggested they get married right away.

"No, it would be more of an act of desperation than a celebration. Let's wait until we know we *have* a future," replied Jill.

The surgery went well, but recovery was slow. Jill spent most of the time in bed or on the living room couch, too weak to do much else. Kyle tended to her every need, and did so with great patience and compassion. She was the love of his life and, although he was not particularly religious, he prayed with great passion for her survival.

Focusing so steadfastly on Jill's situation resulted in Kyle losing considerable weight himself, and his friends took notice.

"You better pay some attention to yourself, or you're going to need someone to take care of you, Kyle," advised his business partner, Sid Haley.

Haley and Kyle had launched a startup company two years earlier and had been having modest success. Now Kyle was concerned that he couldn't give the initiative the necessary energy it required.

"Don't worry, man. Things are going pretty well. The guys at the office got your back, and I sure as hell do, partner," Sid assured him.

Despite, Haley's words, Kyle felt he was letting the nascent enterprise down, but while he could deal with its potential failure, he felt certain the loss of Jill would be his total undoing. *I think she's turning the corner,* Kyle reminded himself, trying hard to be hopeful. Just that morning, Jill's face had shown more color than it had since she'd fallen ill. Furthermore, she had eaten most of her breakfast, a singular accomplishment, considering her morning repast typically consisted of a piece of toast.

"Good for you, babe. Eating like a construction worker."

"I haven't felt this hungry forever," responded Jill, with a smile.

"You're rebounding big time. You look real good. Maybe we can get you out for a walk," suggested Kyle.

"You know, I think I'd like that."

It had been months since the young couple had roamed through their neighborhood, and it filled Kyle with excitement. "Just like it used to be. I know you're going to be fine. Never doubted that."

"Oh yeah, like you never doubted I'd get better, Mister 'life sucks and then you die.'"

"Well, I don't doubt it *now*. It's obvious you're better. You're going to be cured, sweetie, and things will be back on track."

"Hey, bring it down a notch or two, Kyle. Just because I'm feeling a little better doesn't mean I beat the damn cancer. We'll see how things are next week when I get checked at the hospital."

"I told you," shouted Kyle gleefully, when Jill was told her pancreas was still clear.

"We'll do another check in three months, Jill, but I think we have reason to be very happy," said the oncologist, rising to signal that the appointment was over. "Eat well, drink lots of fluid, get plenty or rest, and enjoy life," said Dr. Carlyle, giving her an extended hug.

While Kyle felt tremendous relief, he was hounded by the possibility that Jill's cancer might still return. *That's what cancer does.* His ever-present doubt about their future resulted in his doing something he would never have imagined doing. He had noticed a sign in the window above the local convenience store proclaiming, "Tarot Card Readings." Kyle had always found the idea of fortunetellers and soothsayers ridiculous, but now in his current state-of-mind, he cast aside that skepticism and ventured up the stairs.

Jesus, it's just like in those creepy movies, thought Kyle, as he pushed through the beaded curtain that led into a parlor adorned with astrological charts and posters of centaurs and unicorns.

"Please come in. I was expecting you," said an elderly woman sitting behind a table covered in red velvet.

No crystal ball? mused Kyle, tempted to challenge the woman's statement about expecting him but thinking it better to play along with her. *What the hell? You're here. When in Rome...*

"Sit down, young man. There are things you want to know. Let the cards tell you what you seek to learn."

Looking like she was from central casting, the fortuneteller spread a deck of cards before her and stared at them intently.

I can't believe you're doing this, Kyle. Give her a few bucks and get the hell out of here.

"Your lover has been through a great crisis. Perhaps something life-threatening?"

Kyle was amused by what he figured was just a *very* good guess. "Yes, my girlfriend had cancer but she's okay now."

The old woman turned over another card and grimaced.

"You love her deeply, but there is betrayal in the future. She will give her heart to another."

Kyle stood up suddenly. *This is just a totally stupid idea!*

"Please stay seated," said the woman. "There is more."

"No thank you. I don't believe in this mumbo jumbo," blurted Kyle, tossing what cash he had in his pocket on the table.

"Please, sir, let me continue," pleaded the psychic. "There are other things I must tell you... "

"Goodbye," said Kyle, exiting. "I won't be back."

Betrayal? Bullshit! Not Jill. Never! reflected Kyle, returning home.

Jill continued to regain her former health in the months that followed, and Kyle was thankful and pleased to see her thriving again.

"Dr. Carlyle saved me. I love him. He's so special," gushed Jill. "I wouldn't be here without him... or *you*, honey."

She loves him. Patients fall in love with their doctors all the time, mulled Kyle, immediately recognizing the absurdity of the idea that Jill would hook up with the medico. *She doesn't mean it* that *way, you idiot.*

But the fortuneteller's dark prophecy came to dominate his thoughts, and he found himself withholding more and more affection from her. *She will give her heart to another.* In time, it became difficult for Kyle to even touch her. Although his love for her remained strong, the thought that she could cheat on him left him emotionally paralyzed.

"What's wrong, Kyle? You seem like you're somewhere else. Not with me. Very distant and removed," complained Jill, adding, "I love you, you know."

"I love you, too," replied Kyle, coolly, the ominous prediction of the seer echoing in his head.

"I hope so. You'll tell me if something's wrong, right?"

"Of course I will," answered Kyle, but he did not—nor did he bring up the subject of marriage again.

Months passed in much the same manner, and as the New Year came and went, Jill arrived at the conviction that Kyle had fallen out of love with her. Although this was far from the truth, his ability to demonstrate his real feelings for her was fatally inhibited by his fear that she would leave him for another.

After intense soul-searching, Jill finally reached a decision about the relationship.

"I can't take it any longer, Kyle. You've frozen me out. I don't know why you've changed. You aren't who you were, so there's no reason for us to stay together."

"You're in love with someone else. I knew that was coming," replied Kyle.

"Are you crazy? I'm not leaving you for someone else. I'm leaving you because you've become another person. The person I was in love with died with my cancer. Ever since I've been better, you've been another person. I have to get out of here before I'm devoured by *your* malignancy."

"No... no, I *know* that you've given your heart to another. It was in the cards."

When You Give Too Much, You Leave Yourself Empty

Sympathy is what she said she wanted, so I gave her as much as I had to give.

"It's not enough!" she wailed, storming out of the apartment.

Damn! I thought. *Now what am I going to do without what sympathy I had?*

A Slimy Revenge

Man is Nature's sole mistake.
~ W.S. Gilbert

From the single engine Cessna, the water below appeared pleated like the lining of a ski parka. Discolored snow trickled into Lake Mogg from the hills surrounding it. Dead wildlife cluttered the shoreline having apparently expired as they drank. Predators feeding on the carcasses soon came to the same end next to their convenient feasts. An alarm bell from the vacant Goodman Company building rang continuously, echoing throughout the increasingly lifeless valley. It could be heard up in the small plane circling the factory's towering smoke stack.

"What the hell happened down there? And who set off that alarm?" asked Peter Sampson, the Selby County sheriff.

"Whatever it is, it looks like it's killing everything in its path," replied the pilot, Harvey Beckman.

"It's leaving an oily coating on everything. Jesus, I think I can actually see it move. At this rate, it will hit Curran in about a day. Let's get back. Got to get people evacuated."

"What the hell were they doing at Goodman to cause this?" asked Beckman, banking hard for a return to the town runway.

"Think something besides recycling plastic," observed Sampson, feeling a growing sense of urgency.

Twenty minutes later they landed at the tiny airstrip in Curran. As soon he got in his car, Sampson called the state's emergency management agency to report the toxic flow. To his surprise, he was told that several similar events were occurring throughout the region.

"What is it? Do they know?"

"No, only that it destroys whatever it comes into contact with."

"How's Route 10 to Bayville?"

"Okay, as far as I know."

"Assume the ocean shoreline hasn't been affected?"

"Not as far as we know."

"Well, I'm going to get my people to Bayville then and wait this thing out."

"Roger that, Peter."

All of Curran's 322 residents were summoned to an emergency meeting at the local school, and nearly all attended. Word of the situation had already moved through the small village, and anxiety filled the expressions of everyone in attendance.

"Those of you that have folk who couldn't be here make sure they're told what I'm about to tell you," said Peter. "We got something deadly moving our way and only a limited amount of time to escape its path."

"What is it?" shouted a voice from the audience.

"Not sure. It appears to be some kind of toxic ooze, and it's cutting a wide swath between here and up at the lake."

"It's the Blob," offered Chuck Belmont, half-joking.

"Well, that might be an apt description. It's running over things and killing what it comes into contact with. I estimate it'll reach town in about 14 hours, and that means everybody's got to leave ASAP! Given the direction of the crawling stuff, I think it makes most sense for us to evacuate over to Bayville."

"Is it anywhere else, or just here?" inquired Sue Bathgate, Curran's town administrator.

"I talked to MEMA, and they say that several other parts of the region have reported a similar thing."

"How about out of the state?" continued Bathgate.

"Haven't heard. But wherever else it is, the main thing is that it's about to hit us, so we got to get the hell out of the way... pronto!"

"If anybody needs transportation, I can fit six in my van," offered Belmont.

"We can load up the school bus, too," added Bathgate.

"All right, then. Let's give ourselves an eight-hour window to be out of here, just in case the… *Blob* speeds up. Really, this is serious, folks. A matter of life and death, I'd say, from what we saw out there."

The sheriff's last remark set off a round of whimpers from the gathering, which very quickly dispersed to gather and pack up their things.

The small plane dropped to within inches of the roiling surface and then turned right and lifted.

"It's picked up speed. Can't be more than six hours from town," reported Sheriff Sampson, back to Sue Bathgate in Curran. "We're returning now. No way this thing is going to stop. How's it going there? Are people leaving?"

"Yeah, but not fast enough."

"Well, they better get moving. Spread the word we got real nasty stuff incoming. It's devastating everything in its path."

"Just heard that this is happening all around the country."

"Jesus, what the hell is going on? Anything about what it is?"

"Heard someone say it's coming from down deep in the Earth. Something like lava, but without the heat."

"Well, maybe no heat but something sure destructive in it. We'll be landing in fifteen minutes. Over and out."

As the plane approached Curran, Sampson was relieved to see a long line of bumper-to-bumper vehicles on Route 10 heading out toward Bayville.

"Guess they got the message, Harvey. Let's get this thing on the ground and get our own families the hell out of here.

"Is it going to reach us, Peter?" asked Clare, as her husband climbed from his police SUV.

"It looks that way. You packed? Kids ready? We don't have much time. Should leave right away," answered Peter, giving his wife a quick, reassuring hug.

"This is so crazy. They say it's all over the country. What does this mean?"

"C'mon, let's get the kids in the car and get to Bayville. We'll talk on the way."

The single lane road east was bumper to bumper as residents of Curran made their way away from the noxious crawler.

"Damn!" mumbled Peter, peering at the traffic ahead.

"Use the siren," suggested Clare.

"No, that wouldn't be fair. We're all in this together."

"Yeah, Daddy. Put the whistle on," said the Sampson's eight year-old daughter, Kathy.

"The lights, too," added their 12-year-old son, Tyler.

"This isn't police work, kids, so it wouldn't be right to do that. Just sit back and relax. We'll get to Bayville."

"Is the Flob thing going to kill us, Daddy?" inquired Kathy.

"Blob, baby. It's from a silly old movie."

"Is the *Blob* going to eat us?"

"Not if it doesn't catch us, and it isn't going to catch us, sweetie."

"But, what if it does?"

"It won't, so don't think about it, okay? Read your book or play your game."

"But, what if it does?" repeated Clare, leaning into her husband and whispering.

Peter shrugged her off and nodded at the road ahead. "See, traffic's speeding up. We'll be at the shore in no time."

"And what do we do when we get there, Peter?"

"We'll keep a watch on the toxic flow. If worst comes to worst, we can get on Brett de Silva's boat for Pinewood Island. This thing might not enter the water."

"What if it does? You said it covered Lake Mogg."

"Look, I don't know. Let's not get ahead of ourselves. It may have already stopped moving, for all we know."

"Can you check on the two-way radio?"

"There's no one left back there to talk to."

"I'll call Mother over in Deacon," said Clare, dialing her cellphone.

"She's probably on her way to the shore, too. MEMA has recommended that everybody get to the ocean."

"The call is not going through. There's no service," said Clare, with panic in her voice.

"Don't worry. The cell phone towers are probably jammed with calls. Try again in a few minutes."

Clare did attempt to reach her mother ten minutes later but without success.

"I hope she's okay. We should have picked her up."

"I'm sure she's fine. You know her. She can take care of herself, honey."

"I hope. What if she couldn't get away because of this ... this *thing*?"

"Did the Blob get Grandma?" asked Kathy.

"Of course not, honey. Shush, Clare, okay? Don't make matters any worse than they are already."

An hour later, they pulled into crowded Bayville. "Oh, my God," said Clare, "it looks like everybody in the state is here."

"Mommy, look, it's Grandma!" shouted Kathy.

Sure enough, the elderly woman stood in a crowd lining the town's main street.

"Stop, Peter!" shouted Clare, who leaped from the car and dashed to her mother.

"Tell her to get into the car. We're going to the police station to see Brett de Silva."

"Who is he, Dad?" asked Tyler.

"Bayville's sheriff. Went to the academy with me. He can help us."

"Are we going on the boat, Dad?"

"I think that's the plan. Of course, everybody here's going to try to get to Pinewood Island."

Clare returned to the car with her mother, who immediately embraced Kathy and Tyler.

"Oh, I'm so glad you're here. I was worried I wouldn't ever see you again because that awful thing is going to kill us all."

"That's great to tell the kids, Myrna," snapped Peter.

"I'm sorry, but that's what they're saying. Thousands of people have already died. They say there's nothing anyone can do to stop it."

"Please, Myrna! Let's try to stay positive. It may not be able to move once it hits the ocean, so we'll get to the island. The sheriff here can get us on his boat. It's a big one. I've already talked with him. So, let's go."

Peter suddenly hit the siren and swerved out of the line of traffic.

"Daddy, I thought you said we couldn't do that," blurted Kathy.

Peter didn't answer.

In minutes, the Sampsons arrived at the Bayville sheriff's office. A crowd surrounded the small building, forcing Peter to push his way to the entrance.

"C'mon, guys, let's get inside. Hold onto your sister's hand, Tyler. You okay, Myrna?"

"Don't worry about me," replied Clare's mother, elbowing anyone blocking her path.

A young deputy at the door met Peter and his family.

"Here to see Sheriff de Silva. Let us in, please," said Peter displaying his badge.

The deputy hesitated, and then Peter saw Brett approaching from behind him.

"Let them in, Hank, before the crowd crushes them," said Sheriff Collins.

"Yes, sir."

The deputy quickly pushed the door shut behind the Sampsons as they slipped inside.

"Jesus, man. People are going crazy out there," sighed Peter.

"Can you blame them?" asked Brett, extending his hand to his friend.

"No, not with what's happening. This is my family, Brett. You know Clare. These are my kids, Kathy and Tyler, and my mother-in-law, Myrna."

"Good to meet everyone. Let's go to my office. You kids like donuts?"

The Sampsons followed the sheriff. As they did, Myrna slumped to the floor.

"Mother!" squealed Clare, prompting everyone to turn around.

As quickly as she had fallen, Myrna was back on her feet, although she was swaying and clutching at the wall.

"I'm okay. Just felt a little woozy. Give me a minute, and I'll be as good as new."

"You need more than a minute. Can we get her a place to lie down?" asked Clare.

"A couch in my office. Come in," said Brett, waving everyone inside.

"Now, don't worry about me, Clare. I'm fine now. Don't need to lie down."

The Sampsons found various places to sit in the sheriff's office, and Peter began to ask questions.

"Have you heard anymore from MEMA? I tried to reach them earlier, but no go,"

"Communication links are apparently down. We've been getting through occasionally. Last I heard this rolling wave of shit... sorry, is advancing steadily. Guess it's emerging from fissures all around the world. Some signs that it's less destructive than first thought, but it sure as hell... I mean heck, is doing enough damage. Thousands of casualties... maybe millions."

"So what the hell can we do?"

"Guess they're dropping stuff on it... napalm. That's the last I heard. As I say, telecommunications links are gone."

"No, I mean what the hell are *we* going to do," repeated Peter.

"Everyone's trying to get on boats and head to the island, hoping this crawling crap won't breach the Atlantic."

"So can we... ?"

"Yep, you guys can come on my boat with my family and some others. We'll head out shortly. Got my son guarding it. People are taking over everything that floats."

There was a sudden knock on the door, followed by a voice calling for the sheriff.

"Come on in, Craig," answered de Silva.

A young uniformed officer entered. His face was filled with purpose. "It's about five miles east, Sheriff. I saw it coming. Wall of slimy-looking stuff just rolling over things in its path. Greenish colored. I thought I saw teeth in it."

"It's got teeth, Daddy?" whimpered Kathy.

"Jesus, it sounds like some kind of animal. Oops... excuse my language," apologized de Silva, emerging from around his desk.

"Rate it's going, should be here in a couple hours, Sheriff," said the anxious deputy.

"Okay, clear the office. You guys get to the police boat. I'll see you on the island."

After fending off the frenzied crowd, the Sampsons and de Silvas floated away from the small dock. Jeers and taunts followed them from those left behind.

"Damn, I wish there were enough boats to take everyone to Pinewood, but what the hell can I do? It really comes down to every man for himself," bemoaned Brett de Silva. "I feel like crap bailing out of town, but there's no other choice."

"Are they going to be killed by the Blob, Daddy?" asked Kathy, staring anxiously at the crowd on the receding shoreline.

"They'll be okay, honey. Don't worry."

"They don't stand a chance," replied Myrna. "That thing is just going to ooze right over them and suck them dry."

"For God's sake, Myrna. Be a little more sensitive!"

As the flotilla of escaping vessels gained on Pinewood Island, everyone watched as the effluence began sliding down the streets of Bayville. Despite being at least a couple of miles away, they could hear the screams of those back on land.

"Everyone's jumping into the ocean," observed Sheriff de Silva. "Not sure that's going to do them any good. It took to the water at Lake Moog, you said. Right, Peter?"

"Yeah, it looked like it crept right over it. All kinds of dead animals."

"Oh, God! It's at the water's edge. Those poor people," cried Clare, clutching Kathy and Trevor."

"Wait a minute! Look!" said de Silva.

"Something's happening to it. It's stopping."

"The stuff is reacting to the ocean. It's withering up… and dying. Look, the reaction is spreading. It's all rotting away, flattening and leaving a silvery stain in its wake. Damn, I think the frigging thing must have been a land slug."

"Slug? Didn't know they came that big. Talk about the wrath of nature. What the hell could have caused that?" said Peter, nodding toward shore.

"I'm sorry! It was my fault. I didn't know this would happen!" blurted Tyler, his eyes filling with tears.

"What's *your* fault, son? What are you talking about?"

"A few days ago I found a slug in our yard, and I poured salt on it to see it disappear."

"You did *what?*"

Daylight Moon

Right smack in the middle of the endless sun-washed sky hung the full moon. Its presence unnerved Jason when he first saw it as a child. A moon in the daylight seemed disturbingly amiss and potentially dangerous to him. He had never heard that anything other than the clouds and sun could occupy the blue panoply above the cornfield where he spent endless hours playing among the winged stalks that dwarfed him. Emerging from the husky maze, he caught sight of the displaced orb and froze. He dared not move fearing the alien eyeball might detect him and do him harm. Finally, he gathered the courage to slip back to the sheltered path that had led him to the alien world.

Nice Doggie

It worked with a dim and undetermined sense
of unknown modes of being.
~ William Wordsworth

Wall. Get through...

"Do you think he'll try to escape?

Hit hard. Dig into it...

"No way he could get out of there."

Again. Smash...

"If he does, he'll kill us."

Crush the surface. Tear away...

"He's in maximum security."

It's giving. Loosening...

"He's gotten out before."

Slam. Dig. Break...

"I know, but it wasn't the Supermax."

Quiet. They'll hear...

"He's not like others."

Deeper, go deeper. Dig harder...

"No, he's not."

Inch in. Go further. More...

"He's *not* human. He's the... "

Rest. Breathe. Start again...

"The *what?* You worry too much."

Better. Deeper. Halfway there...

"For good reason. You forget what he did."

They'll pay. Deeper. Dig more...

"No, I haven't. How could I?"

Smell the outside. Near, near...

"He ate her paws."

Almost out. Get them...

"Don't talk about it, please."

One more big push...

"And what about the fire he set?"

There. Through. Open wider...

"He'd have to be the devil to break out of there."

Climb through, now...

"He *is*. Don't you realize that? He *is*."

Get them. Fly...

"That's ridiculous."

Kill them all...

"He wants to finish us off."

Obliterate them...

"We shouldn't have poisoned his... "

Getting close...

"That thing's barking was ruining our lives."

They're in there. Smell them. Flesh...

"It wasn't normal... *natural*. It was something else."

Eat them. Devour them...

"What's that? Oh God!"

Inside. Bite. Rip. Chew...

Here Come the New K Cars

I lie to myself all the time. But I never believe me.

~ S.E. Hinton

By the early 1980s, the little foreign imports were gravely impacting American auto industry profits. Gas prices were up and domestically manufactured vehicles were distained as fuel-thirsty clunkers. That's when Lee Iacocca, innovator of the Ford's Mustang and Pinto, conceived the idea of Chrysler's K Cars—vehicles that were low cost and fuel efficient—to compete against Toyota, Datsun, and Honda. It was exactly what young car salesman Ralph Bunchy felt would change his faltering fortunes.

"They're delivering the first shipment of the new Dodge Aries and Plymouth Reliants tomorrow, honey," declared Ralph to his half-awake wife.

"Wha… ?"

"The K Cars are finally arriving. Remember I told you about them? I'm going to sell a shitload of the new compacts. They're what people want today. Americans don't want to buy imports, but they don't like spending their pay to gas up their Detroit hogs. That's why I haven't been making any sales. Now that's going to change."

"I hope so, Ralphy. We need to get out of this crummy little apartment, and I need some dental work right away. My right side molar has been killing me."

"I know, Annie. Sorry for the way things have been. I've been trying, but the showroom has been empty. And when a customer comes in, it's the senior guys that get to do the sell. The K Cars are going to change that. They're just what people have been waiting for. I'm going to finally get a chance to show my ability because of these babies."

"We got to get new sheets, too. The ones we have are ripping, and they're too thin to sew."

"Don't worry. Things are going to get a lot better starting tomorrow," said Ralph, reassuringly.

"Why do they call them K Cars?"

"Not sure. Think maybe because people get great deals at K-Mart they figured calling them *K Cars* would sound good," answered Ralph, straightening his tie. "Got to get to the lot, hon. Trust me. Everything is going to change after today."

I'm going to be salesman of the year. Sell more K Cars than anyone else. All the old dudes like are the huge gas-guzzlers, mulled Ralph, as he climbed into his luxurious, three-year-old, fully loaded, 8-cylinder Chrysler Fifth Avenue, provided him by his employer. *Love this boat, but just can't sell you.*

The next morning, two car carriers arrived at Prairieland Chrysler-Plymouth and were quickly unloaded. Ralph watched with unbridled enthusiasm as the K Cars were processed and lined up across the front lot.

I'm ready… I'm ready to sell all of you, reflected Ralph, watching from the showroom window as potential buyers slowly began to appear.

"Okay, fellas, get out there and make room for the next shipment."

"These cars are cheap looking, boss," said Al Strombly, the eldest member of the sales force.

"Yeah, they look like a bunch of Nash Ramblers. Nobody's going to want to be seen in those. Not the people we sell cars to," added Bill Ivory, another long-time employee of Prairieland Chrysler-Plymouth.

"C'mon guys. These cars are priced low and get super gas mileage," replied Hal Berwick, the dealership manager.

"They don't need to sell them. I will," said Ralph, noticing a handful of people roaming around the lot.

"Go get 'em, champ," said Strombly, rolling his eyes and smirking.

"Yeah, sell those ugly things. Get them out of here so we can get cars that look like cars," chimed in Ivory.

They're all mine, pondered Ralph excitedly as he headed out to the lot.

By the end of the day, Ralph had sold four K Cars, and was thrilled beyond measure. His fellow salesmen pretended to be unimpressed, but Berwick was overjoyed and showed it.

"Hell of a day you had, Ralph. Come back tomorrow and sell the rest. Big commission check coming your way, fella."

Anne was thrilled with her husband's success, and the couple celebrated his victory at the local Ponderosa Steak House.

"If Bill and Al don't get involved, and I don't think they will, I'll sell all of the Aries models we've got. Honey, if I do that, I'll—we'll—make $400 this week alone."

"Thank heavens! We can move and buy new sheets," said Anne, the glow on her face enough to light up the night.

It wasn't yet noon the next day by the time Ralph had sold three more K Cars. By then his sale colleagues had tried to get in on the bounty, but had failed to make a single sale. During their lunch break, Strombly and Ivory lamented their inability to move any Aries or Reliants.

"So what do you tell them, Ralph, that makes them want to buy these crap cans," inquired Strombly.

"I tell them how the great gas mileage will save them money while helping protect the environment."

"Help the environment? What are you talking... ?"

"Yeah, when cars burn less gas and emit fewer fumes, they don't pollute as much. I tell customers how Lee Iacocca designed the K Cars so that America can regain its place as the number one car manufacturer in the world. I appeal to their sense of patriotism as well as their desire to save money. The K Cars are the best thing to happen to us, guys."

"Says you. I think they make us look like a low budget dealer," complained Ivory.

"Yeah, and you can't sell any real options to make extra dough on a sale, because they're meant to be strip downs," growled Strombly.

"Hey, you guys should listen to Ralph. He knows a good thing when he sees it, and he's lining his pockets big time," chimed in Berwick.

"Naw, I'm going to stick with what Chrysler has been known for all these years… big, classy sedans and convertibles. Not going to peddle them nondescript Jap wannabe crates," replied Strombly.

This pleased Ralph, who gulped down the remains of his tuna sandwich and headed back out to the lot where customers were browsing the remaining Aries. By closing time, Ralph had sold two more K Cars.

"Hey, listen up everybody," announced Berwick, "Young Ralph here has sold nine cars in two days. That makes him our best salesman ever. He beat your old record of seven sales, Al. Good going, my boy. You'll be glad to know another shipment of K Cars arrives tomorrow to replenish the ones you sold."

Ralph hadn't felt so much joy and pride since receiving the Conservation Good Turn Award from the Cub Scouts when he was nine years old. He beamed with pleasure and nodded in appreciation as the clerical and repair staff of the dealership applauded him.

"See you tomorrow, Ralph. It's payday, too, my friend. Think it's going to take me most of the day to tally up your commissions," said Berwick, patting Ralph on the back and winking at him.

That night, the Bunchys had Chinese delivery, and opened a bottle of Cold Duck to commemorate the auspicious occasion.

"Here's to the greatest car salesman in the world," declared Anne, holding her glass high.

"And here's to the beautiful wife of the *greatest car salesman in the world.* That is, the greatest *K Car* salesman in the world. And I'd like to toast Mr. Lee Iacocca for making my dream—our dream—come true. It's his great design for a low cost, fuel efficient vehicle that has made it all possible."

"Yes, to the great Lee Iacocca!" shouted Anne.

As was the case the day before, Ralph was closing on yet his third sale by noon. When he finished the paperwork on the last purchase, his boss told him he was taking him to lunch at the new Sambo's on Central Street.

"Let's go, Mr. K Car King. Let's grab a bite out, while your fellow employees eat their baloney sandwiches," said Berwick loudly for the benefit of Strombly and Ivory in the lunchroom.

On the way to the restaurant, the sales manager plied Ralph with a steady flow of compliments and hinted that a promotion might be in the offing.

"Let's have a cocktail to note this special occasion," said Berwick, instructing the waitress to bring them two martinis.

"Thank you, Mr... ah, Hal. I really appreciate your being so kind to me."

"Look, Ralph. You've been driving that old Chrysler since you've been here. I think you deserve a new car from the showroom, considering you're now our best salesman," said Berwick, smiling.

"Oh, that's not... "

"Of course it is. The least I can do. It's a gesture of appreciation and an appropriate acknowledgment for your outstanding performance."

"Thank you, but really... "

"I'm letting you have use of a brand new K Car. Pick the one you want."

Ralph looked at Berwick aghast. "No way I'm going to exchange my Chrysler Fifth Avenue for one of those boxy little heaps!"

Plumbed

She aspired and then retired.

~ Jean Marlowe

When the judge's votes in the annual "I Am" competition were tallied in Kingsborough Haven, Willow Sweet was declared Most Beautiful Woman in the county. She was not happy with the designation, because she sought to be recognized in another category. More than anything she wished to be crowned Plumbing Queen. Since she was 16 years old, she had apprenticed with her father, a Certified Master Plumber, and she came to love installing, repairing, and maintaining piping systems.

Willow was equally adept plying her quickly evolving skills in different work settings, be they residential, commercial, or industrial. Over the years, she had developed a formidable affection for PVC cutters, crimp tools, and cinch clamps that rivaled the love she once had for her My Little Pony collection.

"Oh, Father, I do not want to be Most Beautiful Woman. What shall I do? My true place is under sinks, behind walls, and in the damp cellars of our village."

"Don't fret, dear Willow. We shall consult with the judges and see if you can decline the award. Although, I cannot recall when such a thing was permitted."

Willow and her father were granted an audience with the lead arbiter of the contest, and they made an impassioned plea to have the decision reversed.

"Well, it may not have been an appropriate decision anyway," said the official, scrutinizing Willow from head to toe.

"What do you mean?" asked Willow.

"Well, seeing you close up, I'm not sure you were the *best* choice."

"How dare you say such a thing to the *Most Beautiful Woman* in the county?" snapped Willow, indignantly.

If a Loving Creator Exists

If a loving Creator exists,
how can there be racists?

If a loving Creator exists,
how can there be disease?

If a loving Creator exists,
how can there be famine?

If a loving Creator exists,
how can there be war?

If a loving Creator exists,
how can there be orphans?

If a loving Creator exists,
how can there be murder?

If a loving Creator exists.
how can there be tsunamis?

If a loving Creator exists,
how can there be cellulite?

Millennial Geography

He thinks Fargo is only a movie.

She thinks Dubai is an invitation to shop.

He thinks London is in *New* England.

She thinks you can drive to Bermuda.

He thinks the Netherlands is in Disney World.

She thinks Greenland is really green.

He thinks India is a Native American tribe.

She thinks the capitol of Paris is France.

He thinks Iowa borders Oregon.

She thinks Bollywood is in California.

He thinks Alabama is in *South* America.

She thinks Illinois is pronounced *Ill-ah-noise*.

He thinks the Mexican Border was a Spanish bookstore.

She thinks The Great Wall of China is an Asian restaurant.

He thinks Budapest is an insect repellent.

She thinks Cologne, Germany, is a fragrance.

He thinks Venus is a city in Italy crisscrossed by a series of cannolis.

She thinks Tiananmen Square is a board game.

He thinks the Black Sea is in Africa.

They think GPS *is* Geography.

Things You Wish You Only Had To Do Once a Year

Get up for work

Visit your in-laws

Weigh yourself

Do your laundry

Clip your toe-nails

Say you're sorry

Pay the bills

Scoop the litter box

Shop for groceries

Clean the bathroom

Shave your legs/face

Mow the lawn

Remove the trash

Take your pills

Wash the dishes

Floss your teeth

Empty your bladder

What the Purse Possessed

Deep from human vanity,
and the pride from life that planned her.
~ Thomas Hardy

While Coach, Gucci, Chanel, and Louis Vuitton had captured most of the high-end women's handbag market, in Florence Earl's estimation nothing equaled the style, beauty, and cache of the *Escalier Sac a Main* by Brul Conte. She had dreamed of owning the fabled handbag and had recently arrived at the conclusion that price be-damned. It was worth every last penny of its $5,300 price tag from her perspective... if not her friends'.

"It's discounted by 40 percent right now. Usually almost $10,000."

"Still, you can get a Chanel Jersey Flap Bag for $2,500, Flo," advised her longtime friend Estelle.

"Nice, but common, my dear," replied Florence, with a dismissive wave.

"Yeah, right. I should be so lucky to have such a *common* bag."

"The *Escalier* is made of Balenciaga leather, and Brul Conte lines their bags with the finest Chinese silk available. No other manufacturer does that. It takes softness to a whole new and exquisite level."

"You've done your homework, girlfriend. But you could put the money down on a car. Your Camry is older than the hills and keeps needing repairs. Just yesterday you were saying the car was driving you crazy."

"So I'll take the bus when it dies. Lately, I usually do anyway. At least I'll look great with the *Escalier* on my arm."

"You take that on the bus, and somebody will cut off your arm to get it."

"Oh, c'mon, I want it and have been saving forever to buy it. You're the one who's always saying you shouldn't deny yourself happiness."

"I put a limit on that. Five grand for a purse is way beyond it. But, hey, it's your hard-earnd money... "

"True, and I'm worth it. So I'll see you tomorrow at work, and if you're less critical, I'll let you touch the most magnificent handbag in the world."

"You're nothing if not generous, sweetie. See you then."

As soon as Estelle left Starbucks, Florence headed to Nordstrom to make her once-in-a-lifetime purchase. On her way, she thought about putting the handbag on her charge card, but then reminded herself that her goal was to buy the *Escalier* using the money she had saved for that express purpose. *Don't go adding to your card. It's already too high. Besides, it's close to its ceiling anyway. Cash it is.*

Her heart skipped a beat when she reached the store's department that sold handbags. *I'm going to do it. I'm going to own an Escalier.*

"May I help you, Ma'am?" inquired a young woman in an expensive suit.

Florence wondered how store clerks could afford costly apparel on their low salaries, and then she wondered if Nordstrom provided their sales staff with clothing during their shifts. *Wow, I bet she has Prada on.* "Yes, I'd like to see the *Escalier Sac a Main.*"

"Of course," said the young woman, reaching under the display counter. "We only have the one style, but I assume it's what you want."

"Indeed, it's exactly the one I want," replied Florence, attempting to quell an urge to squeal with utter delight.

"It's the last one we have, and it's on sale."

"Yes, I know. It's marked down 40 percent."

"I've never seen such a reduction on an *Escalier*. It is magnificent," said the sales clerk, handing it to her customer.

For a moment, Florence thought she might actually faint. Her head swirled with excitement. *Oh, my God. I'm going to buy it... really buy it.* "I'll take it!" blurted Florence, to the surprise of the sales person.

"Really? I mean, of course. Will it be cash or credit card?"

"Cash... ah, check."

"I'll wrap it for you, ma'am."

"No… no, that won't be necessary. I'm going to wear it. I'll transfer my stuff from this little purse, and you can throw it away. It's old. I only brought it because I knew I'd be getting the *Escalier* and wearing it immediately."

"I can do that, ma'am."

Within minutes, Florence was outside and walking down the street with her new purchase on her arm. *I feel like a queen. I just can't believe it. I think people are staring. It's so class…* I'm *so classy.*

"Hot damn, you actually did it! You bought it!" blurted Estelle, when Florence arrived at work the next day.

Florence swung around as if on a fashion show runway. "Isn't it gorgeous?" she cooed, though rather loudly.

"*Shh…* you'll wake the dead. The boss is in," warned Estelle, pointing toward his office.

Florence cupped her mouth and giggled. "I can't help it. I've been so giddy since I got it. I feel like Princess Kate. She has one, you know."

"Yeah, and *she* can afford it."

"You should see the looks I get."

"People always look at crazies."

"C'mon. You're just jealous."

"Well, maybe a little. Let me hold it."

"Are your hands clean?"

"No, I've been dipping them in grease. *Gimme!*"

Estelle held the *Escalier* gingerly and looked through its interior.

"Well," inquired Florence, grinning smugly.

"Yeah, okay, it's beautiful, but I'd still spend the money on something else."

"To each her own. Okay, time's up. Hand it back."

"Hey, my high school reunion is coming up next month. Can I borrow it for that?"

"Not a loaner, sorry."

"Oh, come on," pleaded Estelle.

"I'll think about it, but don't get your hopes up."

Florence took the afternoon off to go to the dentist and get her hair done. At every stop she made it a point to direct attention to her handbag. The response to it was more than satisfying and affirmed the wisdom of her purchase. Every woman she met practically drooled over the *Escalier* and looked at her with envy.

"Oh my God, it's lovely. I've never seen one of these up close," gushed the receptionist at the dentist's office. "They're so expensive. At least $2,000, right?"

Florence gave a little chuckle before enlightening the woman. "Five times that when they're not on sale, and they hardly ever are."

At the hair salon, the reaction to the handbag was equally passionate. Women gawked at the pocketbook with awe and curiosity, adding to Florence's enormous pleasure. *Buying the Escalier was the best thing I've ever done. I wish I could afford another. I'll start saving again. Wouldn't it be wonderful to have two?*

When her appointments were met, Florence decided to forego the bus and walk the ten blocks to her apartment. She had never derived the level of satisfaction as she had showing off her stunning accessory. And stares she got, including those of a scruffy-looking man, who began following her as she neared her address. As soon as she opened the door to her building, moreover, the stranger pushed her inside the entrance.

"Gimme your money, lady, and don't make any noise about it," he ordered.

Florence clutched at her precious handbag and whimpered.

"What you got in there? Empty it out... *now!*"

"You can have my money but not... "

"But not what? You got something valuable in there? Gimme the purse."

Florence groaned as the thief dug through her prized possession. "Thirty-seven bucks. That all you got? What's so valuable?"

In shock and unable to think clearly, Florence literally let the cat out of the bag, "I spent everything I had on it. Please don't take my *Escalier.*"

"Your what?"

"My purse. It's… "

"This cheap looking thing? Why would I want this crap," said the man, returning it to Florence." "You get it at Wal-Mart?"

Florence's anxiety suddenly turned to indignation. "Cheap? Are you a total idiot? This is one of the most expensive… "

"Hey, I know cheap when I see it, and that bag ain't worth nothing. You can keep it, lady. I'd take it for my girlfriend, but she wouldn't want to be seen with it. Got better taste."

"It usually costs $10,000, though I got it for half that at Nordstrom yesterday. If you don't believe me, the receipt is in there."

"You shitting me, lady?" said the man taking renewed interest in the handbag.

"No I'm not *shitting* you," replied Florence, haughtily.

"Well, in that case, gimme it back," ordered the robber, who then ran off clutching the handbag.

"Damn right!" said Florence, shouting after him triumphantly. "It's an *Escalier Sac a Main*. The most beautiful handbag ever!"

Another Lovely Day in Decayville

Dead hair. I got corpse head, sighed Carl Lamont, staring at himself in the bathroom mirror. *Freaking dried up straw.*

The octogenarian ran his index finger down a deep wrinkle leading from the top of his drawn cheek to the dark crevice in his bristly chin. *Withering up like a sun drenched prune. Damn raisin face.*

He then pushed at the bulbous bags under his eyes. *Where the hell did they come from? How come so big? Like face testicles.*

When Carl blinked his drooping lids, filmy liquid ran from the corners of his bloodshot orbs. *Failing tear ducts to join the drippy bladder. Can't stop the body's terminal flow. Everything's running out... letting go.*

He took notice of his ever-growing brows. *Andy Rooney awnings.* And the long white strands sprouting from his floppy ears. *You in there, Rapunzel? Well, get out while the getting's good!*

Finally, Carl inserted his false teeth and spread his thin lips broadly to inspect the result. *Better than just the gummies, I guess.*

"I'm waiting, honey," chirped a women's voice from the other room. "Hope you didn't put your teeth in yet."

"Oh, crap!" grumbled Carl, unplugging his hearing aid.

The Phenomenologist

This barbarous philosophy, which is the
offspring of cold hearts and misunderstandings.
~ Edmund Burke

As a student, Jason Shepard believed that he had discovered a philosophy of life that suited him perfectly. After conducting cursory studies of several prominent philosophies, he'd come to believe that Phenomenology embodied the tenets that would bring him success and happiness. His interpretation of its aesthetic, however, was seriously flawed. Rather than simply "a system designed to study the structures of human experience and a science of phenomena as distinct from that of human nature," Jason perceived Phenomenology as endorsing the full exploration and exploitation of the individual senses.

His egocentric and distorted approach embraced the view that whatever he did in opposition to the natural world possessed transcendent merit and that encounters with members of the human race should expressly benefit *his* needs. This was very different from what the originators and scholars of Phenomenology had intended, but Jason did not seek a clearer understanding. What he wrongfully assumed the doctrine espoused suited his self-serving interests. He had found a strategy on which to base his life.

I'm a Phenomenologist, he repeated to himself, savoring the sound of the exotic term and thrilled by the identity he felt it gave him.

Following college, Jason practiced his distorted version of the philosophy in every aspect of his life. His business degree got him hired at a financial firm in Chicago, and within his first year he had bedded three women in his department. Tensions rose as a consequence, and Jason moved to take a position in Los Angeles as business manager for a television station. There, too, he let his libido rule him and within six months had had intimate relations with the co-anchor of the evening news as well as one-night stands with two other station employees. Soon word was out that Jason was an unconscionable womanizer–a cad–and he had to seek his pleasures elsewhere. He did so with little effort, as his good looks, income, and glib repartee made for easy pickings.

The years passed pleasantly for Jason as he continued to satisfy his needs and desires in whatever way necessary. He made friends but then often exploited them for what he could gain. He practiced deception when it served his purpose. He took everything he could and, if at all possible, avoided giving anything back. It did not matter to him that he frequently wounded those with whom he became involved. Seducing a friend's wife or casting aspersions on the reputation of coworkers in order to get promoted was acceptable behavior in the world as he saw it. What was of foremost importance to Jason was *his* self-fulfillment. He believed that was what living as a disciple of Phenomenology meant, and he was true to its principles, at least as far as he understood and defined them.

At thirty-five, Jason was content with how he had lived his life up to that point, although he could not claim any sustained friendships or relationships. It had not mattered until he met Natalie, when something unfamiliar occurred to him. He fell deeply in love with her. It was not something he had sought, but she captured his heart like no one ever had. For the first time in his life, he dove headlong into the relationship, giving of himself completely. He was a changed man and found himself the happiest he had ever been. During his time with Natalie, he became less self-absorbed and more interested in the feelings of others, especially hers. Whatever he could do to please her, he did enthusiastically and selflessly. Her happiness became his.

After four months of spending nearly every day together, Jason asked Natalie to move in with him and she agreed. In the weeks that followed, Jason slowly grew to realize that his adherence to his idea of Phenomenology had been depriving him of genuine fulfillment.

"I hope you're as happy as I am, sweetheart," gushed Jason, caressing Natalie's naked back as they lay in bed.

"I am," whispered Natalie, sinking into the covers.

"Good, because that's what I want more than anything," declared Jason–himself intrigued by the dramatic change in his attitude since falling for Natalie.

At a gathering held by a couple with whom he and Natalie had become close friends, Jason witnessed something that he first thought must be a hallucination, because it was so inconceivable to him. His friend Mark had gone to the cellar to fetch more wine. He had been absent a long time when everyone took notice of his absence.

"I'll go see what's holding him up," offered Natalie, quickly rising from the couch and going through the glass door that led to the cellar stairs.

Jason noticed her reflection in the panes as she descended the stairs. A few steps down, Natalie met up with Mark. *Good*, thought Jason, whose wine glass had been empty for too long. Then his world was turned upside down as the door's reflection revealed something that shook Jason to his depths. Natalie and Mark embraced and kissed. And this was no casual encounter but one informed by intimacy and passion. For a second, Jason questioned what he was seeing, but he quickly realized that the love of his life was having an affair with their mutual friend.

Jason's first thought was to run to the door and confront them on the spot, but he remained seated, attempting to digest the significance of the incident. *She's cheating on you. How can she be doing that? We're practically engaged. Jesus, I can't believe this. Some friend you are, Mark. All your bullshit talk about fairness and integrity. You frigging phony.*

Suddenly all Jason wanted to do was leave the gathering and confront Natalie. He could not stand being in the presence of the two illicit lovers and trying to pretend that everything was fine when all too obviously it was not.

"Let's go," he whispered to Natalie.

"Why? We just got here."

"I'm tired. I just want to leave."

"Well, you can leave. But I'll stay a while longer. I can get a ride home."

I bet you can, thought Jason, his blood reaching a boiling point. *The two of you can get it on in Mark's car. Screw you and him.* "No, I want you to come home now. I want to talk to you about something. It's important."

"Okay, okay," replied Natalie, growing irritated.

They said little on the drive home, but as soon as they entered their apartment, Jason unloaded.

"I saw you and Mark kissing on the stairs."

"What?"

"In the glass door. I could see the two of you going at it."

"You had too much to drink. We weren't *going at it,"* protested Natalie, removing her coat and heaving it on a chair. "Why are you getting so angry?"

"I have every right to be major pissed. You've been two-timing me and with our friend. That's low, really disgusting. I thought we had something very special."

"If you saw anything, it was an innocent hug. That's all."

"Yeah, right, an *innocent* hug, my ass! You two are involved. Thanks a lot. I trusted you. I can't believe you're doing this to me... to *us.* We have our differences like every other couple, but for God's sake. This is unbelievable. Why are you doing this?"

"I'm not *doing* anything. You're blowing this way out of proportion, Jason."

"You're such a liar, you know that? I know what I saw. I'm not blind. You're a free agent, aren't you? Living with me but screwing others."

"I'm not going to listen to this. Okay, so I kissed Mark. It was nothing. Just a meaningless... "

"Meaningless, my ass. What do you expect from me. I see you and my so-called friend making out and I'm supposed to be fine with it? We had an exclusive relationship... or so I thought."

114

"You don't own me, Jason. I'm sorry you saw what you saw, or what you think you saw. It was just something that happened between Mark and me... spontaneous. There was an attraction and we acted on it."

"So you *do* admit it! Well, no biggie. I was just the man you live with, right?"

"I didn't think... "

"That I'd be upset? Christ, I put everything into our relationship, and you're out there like you were single."

"I am single. We're *not* married."

"You don't get it, do you?"

"Get what?"

"Oh, forget it. You're all about *you*. Just getting what you can and to hell with me. No conscience at all."

"I treated you fine. You're my boyfriend. *Not* my husband. And even if you were, I still have a right to be who I am."

"I know exactly what you are."

"And what on earth is that?"

"You're a goddamn *Phenomenologist!*"

"And what does that mean?"

"Look it up," growled Jason, storming out the door.

After Jason left, Natalie turned in for the night. She slept soundly.

How Close...

I came to obliterating everything–all senses and cells. A picosecond from the death of future moments. How intensely I felt the urge, the need, to strike. To abolish in a delicious fury
you... and me. *Especially* me.

Life's Profound Questions

Do fish prefer to be deep-fried, baked, or consumed raw?

Where does the Bird of Paradise go on vacation?

Can toes be taught to clip their own nails?

Does weather laugh at meteorologists?

Will cancer ever be used to enhance the quality of life?

Does the Earth feel pressure at its core?

Can warts be made to look attractive?

Is the cactus community aware it is full of pricks?

Where can rats find a place they are loved?

Can flies be programmed to eat one another?

Does a political party exist that respects both sides of an issue?

Is famine ever truly fulfilling?

Does asphalt like to be driven over?

Why do alligators taste like chicken?

When does a poem really write itself?

Does granite ever feel weak?

Are slugs moving as fast as they can?

What kind of food does thought like?

Is there ever a perfect case of diarrhea?

First Chills

Memories are hunting horns whose sound dies on the wind.
~ Guillaume Apollinaire

It was apparently naptime. I was maybe three or four years old and lying atop a bed... perhaps my bed. But I'm not really certain. The sheet is pulled down around my waist, and I have no top on. The lace curtain sways from the balmy air drifting through the window. At first I wonder if someone or something is behind it, but I see only the sun's rays seeping through the patterned fibers.

All is quiet except for the warble of the Carolina Chickadee. *Fee-bee-fay-bee* it sings over and over from its perch on the limb of the Angel oak tree that stretches within inches of the house... maybe my house. I'm not really sure about that either. Things don't look as familiar as they should.

The scent of magnolia perfumes the air reminding me of something my mother said... when she was alive. *Eat the bruises in the fruit. They're the sweetest part.* I try, but they taste too soft and wormy to me. Why would she tell me that if it wasn't true? She had many bruises. In her coffin, I could make out one under her jaw, even though it was covered with something to hide it.

Suddenly I hear footsteps from beyond the closed door. Probably Dad's... should be his. As quickly as the thumps occur, they fade and disappear. I turn back to the curtain and watch its fluttery dance. Again, the chickadee's chirps are the only sound in the space around me. Sometimes they remind me of my bedtime prayer–*fee-bee-fay-bee, now I lay me.*

My eyes get heavy and I begin to drift off, but it is then that I feel cold fingers run up and down my back. I let out a squeal as I turn to see who is behind me. There is no one there. *But there was*, I think, absolutely convinced. *There was... I felt something touch me. I did. I know I did.*

The sparsely furnished room offers no clues though. The only explanation my young mind can devise prevents me from lying on my side for most of my childhood to keep that ghost from returning.

Doing a 360 on Route 66

My son, may you be happier than your father.
~ Sophocles

We stand on a strip of steaming asphalt a mile east of Barstow, California. Our thumbs are extended in growing desperation. The desert wind batters our sun-seared skin, as do the dusty contrails caused by the cars streaming by us at high speeds. My dad rages at our situation, cursing our bad luck.

"These jerks don't give a damn about a family trying to get a ride. We could die out here in this God forsaken hole, for all they care."

Same old stuff... Heard it all before, I think. We've been on the road ever since my mom left because of my dad's drinking. He's not as angry when he's drunk though. Sometimes he cries.

A dust devil swirls across the railroad tracks only yards from where we stand and wraps us in its flailing arms.

"Goddamn life!" spits my dad, desperately attempting to restore his wispy hair to its previously slicked back position.

"That was just like a tornado, Dad," I say.

"No it wasn't," he mumbles, gloomily.

"Yes it was," I insist. "Bet we're going to get hit by another. The next one will probably be bigger, too."

"Oh, pipe down, will you, Mick? Jesus! Blab, blab, blab . . . that's all you do."

Another car roars by without even slowing down to check us out.

"See!" growls my dad. "You can't put your faith in people. They'll let you down every time."

I say I know that, half believing my words.

"Son-of-a-bitch!" he shouts at a passing 18-wheeler, whose powerful back draft nearly knocks us over.

My dad removes his upper plate and hacks up a huge glob of brown phlegm.

"Wow, you got mud in your lungs, Dad," I say, as much to goad him as to direct his attention to the sad state of his lungs from smoking two packs of Camels a day.

"Be quiet!" he rips. "I don't need to hear that crap. Things are bad enough without you gabbing on and on."

Another whole hour drags by with seven cars failing to stop and offer us salvation. I'm keeping count. Not much else to do.

"That makes 24 cars that haven't picked us up since we started today," I declare, in an authoritative tone.

"You're going to lose count, kiddo," grumbles my dad, reigniting a half-spent cigarette. "These local yokels are ignorant. They wouldn't give you the sweat off their balls if you were dying of thirst."

Just then a pickup truck slides across the gravel to a stop and its driver flags us on. My dad grabs our canvas bag and we dash in its direction.

"I *knew* we'd get a ride eventually," he proclaims, grinning as we approach our waiting ride.

"How you guys doing?' inquires our rescuer from behind the wheel of his decrepit vehicle.

"Couldn't be better!" gushes my dad. "Couldn't be better!"

About the Author

Michael C. Keith is the author of more than 20 books on electronic media, among them *Talking Radio, Voices in the Purple Haze, Radio Cultures, Signals in the Air,* and the classic textbook *The Radio Station* (now *Keith's Radio Station*). The recipient of numerous awards in the academic field, he is also the author of dozens of articles and short stories and has served in a variety of editorial positions. In addition, he is the author of an acclaimed memoir–*The Next Better Place* (screenplay co-written with Cetywa Powell), a young adult novel–*Life is Falling Sideways,* and seven other story collections–*Of Night and Light, Everything is Epic, Sad Boy, And Through the Trembling Air, Hoag's Object, The Collector of Tears,* and *The Near Enough.* He has been nominated for two Pushcart Prizes and a PEN/O.Henry Award and was a finalist for the National Indie Excellence Award for short fiction anthology and a two-time finalist for the International Book Award in the "Fiction Visionary" category. His books have been published in several foreign languages. www.michaelckeith.com